FIVE THOUSAND POUNDS

Agnes Giberne

Pharos Books

ISBN: 978-93-5983-187-9
eISBN: 978-93-5983-295-1

©Publishers

Publisher: Pharos Books (P) Ltd.
Plot No.-63, First Floor, Main Mother Dairy Road
Pandav Nagar, East Delhi-110092
Phone: +14049995474, 011-40395855
WhatsApp: +91 9319228272
E-mail: sales@pharosbooks.in
Website: www.pharosbooks.in
Edition: 2024

Printed By: Sushma Book Binding House, Okhla
Industrial Area, Phase II, New Delhi-110020

Five Thousand Pounds
By : Agnes Giberne

Contents

C H A P T E R   I

My Cottage Home

UP to the age of fourteen I think I spent as happy a life as any child in any cottage home in England. There is many a cottage which is no "home" at all, in the true sense of the word, notwithstanding those pretty words of poetry about—

"The cottage homes of England,

By thousands in her plains;"

but ours was one.

It stood on a bit of country road, with three or four other cottages, close outside a biggish town. We had a large pond in front, and lots of trees beyond and on both sides of the pond; and the shadows of the trees used to look very pretty on a summer evening, when the light from the sun came creeping through them with a red glow like firelight. The water would catch the glow, till it was all one sheet of brightness, and the trees seemed bending down to look at their own likenesses below, for every branch and twig and leaf might be seen there, pictured.

Sometimes a breeze would ruffle the surface, and then there were little wavelets, with red on one side and grey on the other, and the pictured branches and leaves had a snaky sort of movement in and out of one another. And if a duck swam across, leaving its little track, that made another break in the smooth picture.

I used to stand and watch these things, and wonder at the ripples and the brightness. Sometimes I asked father the "why" of this or that, for I was an inquisitive child, but he always said, "Don't know, my girl," and went off to his pipe; so it was not of much use to ask him. If I put the same questions to mother, she commonly said, "How can I tell? Don't bother!" and that shut me up.

And if I went to grannie, she would say, "Because God made it so, Phœbe." This was all right and true, but I would have liked to understand a little more about the beautiful things which God has made. I used to wonder then, and I often wonder now, how it is that people care so little to look into such matters.

Well, but I must go on about my home, the only home I ever knew in childish years.

It was a pretty cottage. Clematis grew over one side, and in front there was a rose-tree, which used to flower all the summer through and on almost into the winter. The roses were small and white, but how they did cluster! People often stopped to remark on them. We had a nice piece of flower-garden in front, stuffed full of sweet-williams and pinks, and such plain old-fashioned plants: none the less pretty for being old-fashioned, however. At the back there was a tiny strip of kitchen-garden too. The front door had a porch, and honeysuckle grew thickly all over it, with long trailing pieces, which had to be lifted and put aside when we went out or in.

Grannie had lived in this cottage all through her married life, and when her husband died she lived on there still, with her only boy,—my father,—working for him, and making him work for her.

Father's work was in the building firm of Johnstone & Co. We thought Mr. Johnstone a very grand person in our little town, because he was so rich, and wore such a thick gold watch-chain, and had such a big red stone in the ring on his little finger. But I dare say he would not have been thought so much of elsewhere. He was not a gentleman, and he very seldom spoke a kind word to any of his men, as I am sure he would have done if he had been a true gentleman.

Father was not a skilled workman, but he had good wages nevertheless, for he was steady and trustworthy.

He was always kind to us children. I never knew him anything else in those days. Sometimes he would speak up sharp in a passing way, but he never knocked us about or stormed at us, as I have seen men do with their children.

He was not a religious sort of man. He went to Church most Sundays, in the afternoon, to please grannie, and sat and nodded through the sermon. He would have done a good deal to please her, though he wouldn't do one thing which she wanted, and that was to leave his bed early enough for the morning Service—no, not even for her sake.

No, father was not religious. If he had been—not merely religious outwardly, but really serving God in his heart—I think our life after might have been different from what it was. It always seems to me, looking back, that poor father was like a fine ship at sea, without any rudder. For a while it may float along quietly enough, on a calm sea and with a fair wind. But let the wind change and grow strong, and it is carried helplessly away and cast upon the rocks. If he had had the rudder, yes, and the Pilot on board, the breeze would have been only for his good. But he had not.

I have many a time had this thought about poor father. He was such a kind man in those days, and so steady. He liked his pipe and his glass of beer, it is true, but he didn't go to excess with either, and he loved his home and seldom went to the public. He brought his wages straight home to grannie always; for it was grannie who managed things, not mother. They were very unlike each other. Grannie liked work, and mother couldn't abide it. Grannie could not be happy without everything neat and nice about her, and mother did not care how anything was. Grannie had always managed everything before father married, and she kept it on after he married. Mother did not mind. She liked to be saved trouble.

Mother was a pretty little woman, with blue eyes and a nice smile. But she was always untidy. Even grannie could not cure her of her untidiness. I don't know what the house would have been like, except for grannie: but that made all the difference. She never let a speck of dust lie anywhere, and she was a beautiful cook.

Grannie set herself early to train me into her ways, and I think I took after her naturally. "You know, Phœbe," she used to say sometimes, "if anything happens to me, it will all come upon you. Somehow, your mother doesn't seem to have the knack; and if somebody else beside her didn't keep things straight, there would be a terrible muddle. Maybe she would not mind, but your father would, and it's a terrible thing to live in a muddle. So see you do your best to learn."

I did do my best, and I think she found me an apt scholar. By fourteen years old I could turn-out tidy little dinners without any difficulty, and I was a capital hand at cleaning up; and as for sewing and darning, I don't really think there was another girl in the place who could have surpassed me.

I was a good deal more grannie's child than mother's. Mother cared most for Asaph. There were only two of us, and Asaph was two years younger than me. He was very like mother in looks and ways, little and pretty, with blue eyes and curly hair, and a sort of easy soft way of doing things. But he was not so easy as not to like having his own way, and he didn't take it softly if anybody crossed him. He loved to lie in bed too, and he hated lessons and work. And mother indulged him right and left. Grannie seldom meddled about Asaph, for it almost always raised a storm if she did.

Grannie was getting on in years, and her hair was white, but she still looked hearty and strong, and was very active and ready to help in many ways. She was religious and no mistake. It was religiousness of the right sort with her—not only going to Church and saying her prayers, as with some people; and not only talking good, as with some other people. She did go to Church of course, and I never knew a more regular Church-goer than she; and she did say her prayers regularly too. And I don't mean either that she could not talk if occasion served. We can generally speak now and then of the things we love best. But her religion didn't consist only in Church-going or in talk. She lived altogether to God and for God, and I don't really think she ever took a single step without considering first whether it was what God would have her do.

C HAPTER II

News

I REMEMBER so well one particular Sunday evening. It is not surprising that I should remember that Sunday evening, for it came just before a great event in our lives.

We had been to Church twice as usual, Grannie and I. Mother never would go in the morning. She said she had too much to do—though really it was not she who did the work. Father lay in bed late, and Asaph followed his example. Grannie and I always got up particularly early on Sunday morning, that we might have everything straight in time for the Service. Grannie always gave father a good cold dinner on Sunday. She had been a servant in a rich gentleman's family when she was young, and she used to say that if the gentleman and his family always had cold Sunday dinners, for the sake of saving Sunday work to their servants, she didn't see why we shouldn't do the same, for our own sake. We were not like the neighbours in this, and father sometimes grumbled a little in a good-tempered way. But he had been brought up to it from boyhood, and the dinners were always so nice that he could not say much. The only things ever spoilt were the potatoes and greens, which mother used to have in charge to cook, as they of course had to be hot. I fancy she often went out for a gossip with the neighbours, and forgot them. If mother would have gone to Church, grannie would have stayed at home, or made me stay at home, to do what was needed. But grannie always said she would not consent to have two kept away from God's House, where one was enough. And grannie could be very firm, when once she had made up her mind.

So we had been to Church in the morning, and then we had all had a nice dinner of beautiful cold pie, good enough for the Lord Mayor's table, and a sort of cold custardy pudding with jam and pastry round. It looked grand, and father was very fond of it, but it did not cost much money, though it did cost a deal of time and trouble in the making. Grannie never grudged time or trouble, however.

In the afternoon we had been to Church again, and father and Asaph with us. Father was a very respectable-looking man in his Sunday suit, and Asaph was such a pretty boy. He looked more like ten than twelve years old, though. Mother would not go with us, for she had toothache. She was a good deal given to toothache, but I think it came oftenest on a Sunday.

The sermon that afternoon was about Temptation. I often thought after, how strange it was that Mr. Scott should have preached it just then.

"Lead us not into temptation" was the text. Mr. Scott spoke a great deal about the meaning of the word Temptation. He said it had two quite different meanings—one was, enticing to evil, and the other was, testing or trying. He said that God never "tempted" any man in the first sense—enticing to do wrong. But he said also that God very often tempted us in the second sense—trying our faith, testing our strength, putting a pull on the rope, as it were, to show how heavy a weight it could bear.

Then Mr. Scott talked about different ways in which God "tempts" people—sometimes by sending sorrow; sometimes by giving pain; sometimes by putting them into difficult circumstances; sometimes, and Mr. Scott made a good deal of this, by letting them have all they most like and wish for. I think that part of the sermon struck me most. It seemed so strange to think of happiness being temptation. But I saw grannie nodding her head with a pleased look, so I was sure he must be right.

Mr. Scott was a good loving-hearted old man, and he was what is called an able preacher. Everybody in the place loved him, for he was a friend to everybody—so far, at least, as people would let him be.

I could not make out whether father was listening to the sermon. He never did as a rule, but used to settle himself into his corner and fall into a half-doze. Sometimes grannie would poke him gently to rouse him, and he would give a great start and make believe to pay attention, but it never lasted long.

This day, however, he really did listen. For in the evening, when we had had our tea, and father and grannie and I were sitting outside the door, as we often did of a summer evening, with the pond in front glistening, and the ducks swimming to and fro, father said—

"I didn't hold with Mr. Scott this afternoon. If good times are a temptation, they're a rare sort to most folks. I think it's trouble that makes one go wrong. I shouldn't mind having a little more of the other, for my part."

"Times aren't bad with us, Miles," said grannie.

"Maybe not, but I shouldn't mind 'em being better," said father. "I shouldn't mind a bit more of holiday now and then—and to take things easily and have less to do."

It was not at all astonishing that father should have made these remarks just before what was coming, for he very often did make them. A week seldom passed without his saying such things.

"I shouldn't wonder if a time of ease and idleness was one of the sharpest temptations God ever sends," grannie said quietly.

Father said, "Now, mother!" in a protesting sort of way.

"I shouldn't," she said, quite firm, and looking him in the face. "Satan has a deal better chance with idle folks than with busy ones, Miles."

"Ah, so you've told me many a time," said father. "And maybe you're right. I don't say but what you are. I'm not an idle sort of fellow myself, by any manner of means. But I don't say I wouldn't like more ease. And as for calling pleasure and riches and that sort, temptation, I don't see it—I don't really see it."

"No," said grannie. "There's many a thing a man can't see, till God gives him sight."

"And you think you've longer sight than me, mother?" says he.

She looked up, with a smile which I thought quite beautiful—looked up, not at him, nor at the trees, but away and above and beyond, as it were.

"Yes," she said; "I've longer sight than you, my dear. I've sight to see up and up into heaven itself, and you haven't. It makes a deal of difference."

"Bless me, mother, don't talk like that," says father, in a sort of hurry. "It sounds as if you was going to die this very night."

"And if I was, I'm ready," said she. "It wouldn't be grief to me to hear the chariot wheels coming near."

But I was sitting close by, and I turned and said, "Grannie, please don't want to go just yet."

"No," she said, "I'm willing to wait."

"Well, you go beyond common folks, somehow," father said. "There ain't many that care to talk about dying as cool as you do."

"No," she said. "And I couldn't either, if death was to me what it is to many a one, a plunge into the outer darkness, away from the smile of God. That would be awful."

"Well, well, we needn't talk about it now," father said, fidgeting. "You're the best woman that ever lived, though you don't think yourself so. But all the world can't be like you."

And he got up, and hummed a tune, and plucked a bit of sweet-william, and walked about; so grannie could not say any more.

The next morning broke like other mornings, and we began the day as usual. Father went to his work, and Asaph to school, which he was nearly done with. This was washing morning, so I was very busy. Mother said her tooth ached still, and she did not seem to think she could do anything. Pain always upset her, and she cried over it half the morning, and went out in the garden and chatted with Mrs. Dickenson most of the other half.

Mrs. Dickenson was our left-hand neighbour, a cleanly thrifty sort of body, but a great talker. She never could resist a gossip, though she worked hard between whiles. Grannie did not like her very much. She had only one child.

In the middle of the day father came back. That was quite unexpected. He always took his dinner with him, and ate it at the works. Grannie used to put it up for him nicely in a piece of paper, with a clean red handkerchief outside. Sometimes it was only bread and cheese, but more often she managed for him to have a slice of cold meat too.

This Monday, instead of staying away as usual, he came home. Our first thought was that he must be ill; but he was walking fast and looking quite red in the face, so it did not seem like illness. Then we fancied that perhaps he had got into trouble and been turned off; but no, he looked too pleased. I had never seen father look so pleased and delighted before. He came hurrying up to us, as we waited at the cottage door, for mother had called us all together in a fright, to see what was wrong, the moment she caught sight of father walking along the road. He hurried up, as I say, and seized Asaph, and gave him a sort of twirl round, like a man in such spirits that he scarce knew what to do with himself. And then he said—

"Guess what's happened?"

"I know," mother said. "You are going to have higher wages."

Father chuckled, and said, "No."

"It's a half-holiday at the works," said grannie.

"No, it isn't. I got leave to run round for five minutes, that's all."

"Then what has happened?" cried mother, and we all chimed in. Grannie was the quietest, and I think she looked a little anxious.

"You want to know, don't you?" says father, chucking Asaph under the chin; "don't you?" and he chucked me too. "Well, I'll tell you. I'm to have Five Thousand Pounds!"

Grannie looked as if she fancied him gone mad. Mother shrieked and clapped her hands, and Asaph copied her.

"Five thousand pounds!" father said again.

"Who's given it to you, my dear?" asked grannie.

"Nobody. It's left to me in a will. Old Andrew Morison is dead, and he has been storing up his money for years, and he quarrelled with his son just at last, and willed it all away to me. Think of that! Five thousand pounds, Sue! Think of that! Five thousand pounds, mother!"

"It's the temptation," said grannie very low, and I heard her sigh.

"It's just lovely," cried mother. "Why, I can have a silk dress."

"Six, if you like," said father. "And Phœbe, too."

I don't know what I said. I felt all in a maze.

"Miles," said grannie, in a trembling voice, and she laid her hand on his arm. "It's a solemn charge for you. Don't you think we ought just to kneel down, and thank God, and ask Him to teach us how to spend it? It'll do us no manner of good without His blessing alongside."

"So you can, mother," said he, all in a hurry, giving her a kiss. "So you can. I'm due back at the works, and mustn't wait. We'll talk it over in the evening, by-and-by. And Sue shall have her silk dress as soon as ever she likes. It makes a man feel all dazed to think of! Five thousand pounds!"

And he was gone. Mother ran away to tell the neighbours, and grannie took me upstairs into the little room which she and I had together. She didn't make but a short prayer, only it was one which I never could forget.

C H A P T E R I I I

The Money

"Who told you about it, Miles?" asked grannie at tea-time. Father had come back, and we all felt very much excited still, as was only natural, I suppose. Grannie looked sad, I thought, but she was the only one to seem so. I had had a restless feeling on me all day, which made it difficult, to settle to work. I don't think I should have settled to it at all, but for grannie's being so bent upon everything going on just the same as usual. She would not abate one jot of cleaning and washing and scouring for herself or for me. But mother did nothing whatever the whole day, except stand at the door, and talk to the neighbours. The news spread quickly, and numbers came to ask what it meant. Some seemed really pleased for us, but they were few. The greater number, as far as I could tell from scraps of talk which I heard in going to and fro, were more inclined to be jealous, and to wonder why such good fortune should have come to us and not to them.

And at tea-time grannie put the question,—"Who told you about it, Miles?"

"Why, it was the lawyer who had the making of the will—a Mr. Carver. It was him and young Mr. Johnstone," father said. "The lawyer came over by train from Lanston this morning, and he told Mr. Johnstone first, and then they sent for me and told me. Mr. Johnstone said I was a lucky man, and he shook hands with me—first time he ever thought of doing that."

"Young Mr. Johnstone isn't near so stuck-up as his father," mother said.

"He's more of a gentleman," added grannie; "that's why."

"There's room for him to be," said father. "Well, he told me I was a lucky man, and Mr. Carver talked a deal. I was so dazed at the news, I didn't half take in all he said. Something about saving and investing and stocks,—I don't know what it was."

"I think you'd be wise, Miles, to ask him to say it again, and to take his advice," said grannie. "He knows more of such things than we do."

"Oh, I'm not so sure," says father, thrusting his hands into his pockets. "I'm not at all so sure of that, mother. He's a lawyer, and he'd like to have a finger in the pie, I don't doubt. But I don't want any of my five thousand pounds to stick to his fingers. He's too sleek and smooth-spoken by half for me. I don't trust him."

"Then you'll ask Mr. Scott," said grannie.

"I'll think it over," says father. "No need to be in such a hurry. Time enough to make up our minds."

"I'll tell you one thing that is on my mind," said grannie, speaking slowly, and looking at us all round in turn. "What about the poor fellow who was expecting five thousand pounds from his father, and who hasn't got it?"

"Jem Morison! Ah, poor wretch, yes," says father in an indifferent sort of way.

"He shouldn't have offended his father," said mother. "But I am glad he did."

"It's sorrowful work for him," said grannie.

"Well, he took his choice," father said. "He married against his father's will, and now his wife's sickly, and they've got twins, and he is in bad health, and can't work. Oh, I dare say he's sorry enough. Most people are when they've taken their own way and have to suffer for it. 'Marry in haste and repent at leisure,' you know. But there's another saying quite as true, and that is, 'It's an ill wind that blows nobody any good.' If young Morison hadn't gone against his father, we shouldn't have this fine windfall. I declare, mother, I don't think you half take in how good it is. Five thousand pounds! Why it'll do anything! Sue is going to be a lady now."

"Fifty thousand pounds wouldn't make a lady of one who wasn't so in herself," said grannie quietly. "Wearing a silk dress is not being a lady, Miles, and you know that as well as I do. I've no wish to see Sue a lady, nor you a gentleman. All I want is to see you both living for God in that station of life where He has put you."

"Well now, mother, you won't go for to say it isn't God who has given us this five thousand pounds, I suppose," says father sharply.

"Yes," she said, "I know He has, and I thank Him for it. But it's temptation, Miles."

Father laughed out loud.

"It's temptation," repeated grannie. "It may be very sore temptation, Miles. I think I'd almost sooner have seen you with temptation of the other sort,—with having too little, instead of too much—if God had willed to send it. I'd have feared less for your being led astray by it."

"Now, mother, you do take a very melancholical view of affairs, and that I must say," protested father. "And what's more, I don't think it's kind. Just because something good has come for once in our lives, you must needs croak about it, and wish it was something bad instead."

"Grannie would like us all to sit down and cry," said mother.

She and father often called her "grannie" just as we children did.

"No, I don't want that, Sue," said grannie. "But I'd have you thankful to God, my dear, and I'd have your eyes open to danger—that's all. And there's one more word I must say, though I'm afraid you won't like it. Seems to me, Miles,—"

Grannie made a stop. "Seems what?" asked father.

"Suppose we were in the place of that poor young Morison, and he was in your place—how do you think you would feel?"

"How? Why, I should count myself an uncommon fool, to have thrown away five thousand pounds for the sake of a pretty face," says father.

"I shouldn't wonder but you'd feel too you had a sort of right to the money, and that the other man hadn't any right to it at all," grannie said.

Father burst into another loud laugh, but it wasn't a happy or a merry laugh.

"Oh, that's what you're driving at, is it?" said he. "No, no, grannie—no nonsense of that sort for me. I'll keep the money fast when I get it. As Morison has sown, he may reap. He's nothing to me, nor I to him."

"He and you are cousins born," grannie said. "Your father's father and the mother of the old man that's dead were brother and sister."

"So much the better for me," father answered. "If I hadn't come next in blood-relationship, old Morison wouldn't have willed the money to me. But it's little enough we owe to any of them in the past, you know, mother. Why, dear me, the Morisons have counted themselves a deal too grand for many a year to have to do with such as we."

"The more reason to be ready to show them kindness now," says grannie.

Father repeated the word "kindness" in a rough sort of way. "Why, you don't really think," says he, "that any living man would be such a born ass as to give up five thousand pounds of his own free will!"

"If he saw it right! Yes, there have been such things done," grannie said, with a kindling in her eyes. "But I would be content if you would give him half, Miles."

Father brought down his clenched fist on the table, with a bang which made the cups and saucers rattle.

"I'll not do it," he said. "I'll not give him one half, nor one quarter, nor one tenth—no, nor one shilling of the money. It's mine, and I'll keep it. Why, bless me, the world would be upside down altogether, if such notions as yours got followed out. You've a sort of craze, grannie, with your religious ways, and that is how it is. But you needn't hug this notion, nor speak of it to anybody. Morison is not going to have one shilling of the money."

C H A P T E R   I V

Congratulations

THE next few days were very stirring. People were always coming in and out, to talk over our "piece of good fortune." Neighbours kept dropping in to congratulate us, and to ask particulars, and to find something more to gossip about. And mother liked nothing better than to talk with everybody about what had happened, and to boast of all that she and father meant to do with the five thousand pounds, as soon as ever it came to us.

"Of course you won't stay any longer in this little cottage," one said. I heard her, and I thought the words were said sneeringly. I didn't like the person who said them—Mrs. Raikes, the wife of a tailor who lived near. But mother took up the idea, and could talk of nothing else for hours. Grannie said quietly—"If you go, you and Miles, I don't go with you;" and she said no more.

I think we all expected the money to come in one or two days, and it disappointed us to hear that we might have to wait a good while. Young Mr. Johnstone looked in one morning, and he was very agreeable and kind. Mother asked him how soon we should have the money, and he said the lawyers were not bound to pay it in less than a year. "I dare say you won't have to wait quite so long," he said, "but lawyers never hurry themselves. And meantime, it isn't at all impossible that the other party may dispute the will, which might cause further delays."

Mother pouted, and was very vexed to think of having to wait. She had so set her heart on having a silk dress directly. But grannie seemed rather pleased than otherwise to hear of delay, for she thought it would give us all time to come to our senses.

Another day, to our great amazement, the Johnstones' carriage stopped at our door. It was a very big heavy carriage, and the coachman and footman were big heavy men, with powdered hair, and a great deal of red and yellow about them, and dangling cords and tassels. I always thought the carriage must be a little like the Lord Mayor's coach. Lord Wheatstone's carriage, which sometimes passed our door, didn't make half so fine a show, for it was plain and dark, and the coachman and footman wore plain dark liveries too—only there was a coronet painted on the door, and the horses were such splendid spirited creatures. I liked the dark carriage best, but father called it shabby beside the Johnstones' carriage.

Well, as I say, the Johnstones stopped at our gate, and mother was quite in a flurry, and went hurrying into the garden, with her cap all on one side. Mrs. Johnstone did not get out, for she was so extremely stout that moving was a great trouble to her. She was dressed in bright ruby-coloured velvet, and a jacket to match, and she had a sweeping straw-coloured ostrich feather on her bonnet, and yellow kid gloves. It looked grand, but I could not quite admire the red and yellow together, though mother thought them lovely. Mrs. Johnstone kept her talking for some minutes, and seemed to think a deal of our "good fortune," as she called it. Mother's head was quite turned, and she could think and talk of nothing for the rest of the day but velvets and silks and feathers. I suppose that sort of taste is catching. I remember looking at my print dress, and thinking how much I should like a pretty new frock. And just after doing so, I caught grannie's eye, and she said—

"Feathers don't make the bird, my dear."

"I do like pretty things, grannie," I said.

"So do I, Phœbe," she answered. "But nothing ever looks pretty out of its right place."

"Would a nice new frock for me be out of its right place?" I asked.

"No, not a nice one, perhaps," she said—"if it was the right way of spending the money. But a smart one would. Don't be easy taken in, my girl. If Mrs. Johnstone was a true lady, she wouldn't be driving about in that dress."

"Wouldn't she?" I said.

Grannie laughed, and said—"Think of Mrs. Scott now, Phœbe. Would she?"

"O no," I said. "But then Mrs. Scott always does dress so quiet."

"Well, think of Lady Wheatstone. You've seen her pass, many a time. Would she?"

"No," I said. "But then it isn't her way to put on such smart things. I suppose she doesn't like them."

"That's just it," says grannie. "She don't like them, and Mrs. Scott don't like them, and if Mrs. Johnstone was a true lady she wouldn't like them either. I don't say but what she may be a nice enough person in other ways, if she does make mistakes in her dress. But they are mistakes, Phœbe. That red velvet, with all the smart trimmings and the yellow feather atop, would do well enough, maybe, if she was going to a Queen's drawing-room, or a Parliament opening, or something of that sort, but they are not fit for driving about in a little place like this. It's just as out of place for her, as if I was to go trudging about in the mud with a green silk dress on."

Mother had been talking about buying a green silk dress for herself that very morning. But grannie had not heard her; if she had, she would have taken right good care not to say words which should seem like blaming a mother to her child—and I would not tell grannie.

Another day our clergyman, Mr. Scott, came. He was an elderly man, with silver hair, and a thoughtful way of speaking, and bright eyes which seemed to look one through. Father was at home when he called. Mother slipped away into the back garden, when she saw him in the distance, for somehow mother never much cared for Mr. Scott. But grannie did love him, and look up to him. She made him sit down in the best chair, and looked as pleased as possible to have him there.

Of course the five thousand pounds were soon spoken of. Mr. Scott told father first how glad he was to hear the news, and how nice it was for us all. He said it in such a kind way, that father was quite pleased. And then Mr. Scott asked father what were his plans.

"Well, I don't just exactly know," father said. "I'm meaning to take a bit of a holiday for one thing, and I did think it would be nice to have a bigger cottage than this: but mother says she'll stick by the old place, and I'm loth to part from her; so we'll wait a while. I've a mind to get some tidy furniture, though, and my wife has a great notion of a silk dress. And we'll have a trip to the sea some fine day."

Mr. Scott listened to all this, and smiled, and didn't seem to think of blaming anybody or anything. I thought grannie was a little disappointed. But presently, somehow, he was talking quietly to father about investing the money, and asking him what he meant to do. For of course five thousand pounds could not be left to lie about, he said, and it was a large sum to put into a county bank. Suppose the bank should fail. Such things did happen.

"Mr. Carver did say something about investments," father said. "But I don't know as I paid much heed. You see, sir, he is a lawyer, and they do say lawyers have a wonderful trick of keeping back some of the money that slips through their fingers;—though, for the matter of that, so have most people."

"You cannot expect them to work without payment," said Mr. Scott. "A lawyer has his living to get, as well as any other man. Of course there are honest and dishonest lawyers; but Mr. Carver is one of the honest sort. He is an honourable man, and you may quite rely on his advice."

Then Mr. Scott talked about different ways of "putting out money," as he called it. I heard such words as "stocks," and "shares," and "railways," and "interest." Father exclaimed presently,—"Only four per cent! That wouldn't be much."

"It would bring you in a nice little income of two hundred a year," said Mr. Scott. "Better have that secure, than aim higher and perhaps in the end lose it all."

"Why, Bill Jenkins told me I'd ought to have ten per cent at least," said father. "And that 'ud be an income of five hundred a year. I was counting on five hundred, so as we could live easy."

Mr. Scott shook his head. "Too much," he said. "Ten per cent is far too high for safety, Murdock. Take my advice, and don't risk your capital where such high interest is given. Four per cent, is likely to be safe. You might even go safely as high as five per cent perhaps, but that is doubtful."

Father did not much take to the notion. He had been talking so big, and making so much of the thought of five hundred pounds a year, that two hundred a year seemed small in comparison.

CHAPTER V

First Purchases

DAYS went by, and still the money did not come. Father grew chafed and restless waiting for it, and mother was in a state of constant ups and downs. Every morning we were keeping watch on the post, and every morning we were disappointed afresh.

"It's no manner of use to be so impatient," grannie said sometimes. "You know right well, Miles, that the lawyers are not bound to pay you short of a twelvemonth, and nobody thinks they'll do it yet awhile."

"Then they ought," father made answer very hotly: for he was getting hasty and not near so pleasant in his ways as he used to be. "We ought to have the money now directly. Not pay for a twelvemonth, indeed! It's my money, not theirs. What right have they to keep us waiting?"

But of course we had to wait all the same, whether he was vexed or no.

It was wonderful how folks ran after us in those days. I had not known before that we had one quarter so many friends. The neighbours were for ever dropping in to talk of our good fortune, and mother seemed such a favourite with them all. I could not help thinking that the money had a good deal to do with her being so, else why should they have cared so little about her before we heard of the five thousand pounds? Grannie felt the same about it that I did, I could see plainly enough, but mother did not. She took it all for real, and was delighted.

A great many asked us out to Sunday dinners, and did their best to give good fare. We hadn't been used to going out on a Sunday to dine, for grannie had always set her face against the custom, and father had only once in a way done it. But now he said it would seem stuck-up and unneighbourly to refuse, just when this "windfall," as he called it, had come to us. He said it would look as if we counted ourselves too grand for the neighbours.

Grannie told him the real question lay deeper; for it wasn't a question of giving offence to one or two people, who ought to know us better than to be so easily offended, but of breaking God's holy day. But father was not to be persuaded, and he and mother went out Sunday after Sunday, and took Asaph with them. And, somehow, after father had been out pleasuring all the afternoon, he did not seem inclined to go to Church in the evening, as he had been always used to do; and one day and another he found some excuse for staying away. I could see that it was a great grief to grannie.

I did not go to these dinners with father and mother, but kept grannie company at home. It was grannie's wish, and mother did not care, for Asaph was her favourite. I don't think I always quite liked being the one left behind, and yet I should not have been happy doing anything else. But if I did not like it, I took care that grannie should not see what I felt. She was sorry enough already about the break-up of our old quiet Sundays.

One day father came in, chuckling and laughing, and carrying a big bundle under his arm.

"What d'you think I've got now?" says he. "O Miles! has the money come at last?" shrieked mother.

"No, it hasn't," said he. "Why, you don't think surely that I'd be carrying five thousand pounds rolled up into a bundle like this! No, it isn't the money, but it's something. And it don't so much matter now, if the money should be longer coming. They'll trust me down at Trowgood's for anything I want. Trowgood himself came up to me in the street, and told me so, as civil as could be. So I went straight off with him, and did some shopping."

"I don't like Mr. Trowgood, and I never did," said grannie. "He's a deep one, Miles."

"Maybe so, maybe no," says father. "Deep or shallow, that won't keep me from using his goods, if so be they suit my wants. And nobody could speak more civil than he did, anyway. Look here, Sue."

Father untied the bundle, while we all stood round. I saw grannie shake her head softly to herself, once or twice, as if she didn't like it at all. But we children could not help thinking the big brown-paper parcel very delightful, for we had not seen many such in our lives. And when it was rolled open, mother quite screamed with delight at the first thing her eyes fell on. For there on the top lay a quantity of smooth bright shining green silk. I almost thought mother would say it was too bright and shining for her. But she did not. She only laughed and clapped her hands, and seemed half beside herself.

"That's the thing now, isn't it?" says father. "Green was the colour you wanted, Sue, and I've chosen the smartest I could see in all the shop, so as you should look your best. You'll have to get it made up quick, and we'll have some folks in to dinner, to look at you. Why, I shall hardly know you, I declare, nor anybody else either. See here! I've bought a real coral necklace for Phœbe. Isn't that pretty, my girl? And here's a cap for Asaph. And I haven't forgotten you, mother. I knew you wouldn't like a green dress, and I had my doubts if you'd wear a silk; so I've chose some good black stuff,—merino, Trowgood says, and the very best they have. You'll wear that to please me."

"Why, it looks like mourning," mother said.

"Grannie never will wear anything but black for her best, and I wanted to get what she'd use," says father.

Grannie was feeling the merino between her finger and thumb.

"It's beautiful stuff," she said—"the best I ever had. And I'm much obliged to you for thinking of me, Miles. It's like your kind heart. But I'd sooner you had waited till the money was come. Supposing it wasn't to come after all, how would you pay for these things?"

"Oh, nonsense, mother,—bother!" said he. "The money's sure."

"Maybe so," said she. "But I'll wait to have my dress made up till it does come."

"I shan't wait," mother said, tossing her head back.

"I shall," grannie said. "I'm obliged to you, Miles, but you'll please to remember that I'm not going to have anything else got for me at all, till the money has come. I don't think it's right. I would send this back straight to Trowgood's, if I wasn't afraid of vexing you."

"It would vex me too," father said. "That's a nice sort of gratitude, I do think. It would vex me, mother, and what's more, Trowgood never takes back cut goods. So you'll just have to be content, and if you're a wise woman you'll get it made up, and wear it when Sue wears her green silk."

"But haven't you got anything for yourself, Miles?" asked mother, looking as pleased as a child over a new toy.

"Haven't I?" said father. "Dear me, yes, a whole new suit. It isn't made up yet, but it soon will be. And I've got a brand new sofa for the parlour, and a clock for the mantel-shelf,—cheap enough, but Trowgood says it'll go like a twenty-guinea clock. Oh, we'll have things smart now, and no mistake. Anything else you want me to get, Sue?"

"I'd like a new cap," mother said. "I saw a beauty to-day, in Trowgood's window, all over pink bows. And I do want a new bonnet for Sundays. I'm sure I should go to Church ever so much more regular, if I had a decent bonnet to show myself in. Mine's got washed strings, and the flowers are all faded. And wouldn't it be nice if we were to get a new carpet for the parlour, and put up the old one in a bedroom? The pattern's all trodden out, and it never was anything but a dingy fright. I should like something nice and bright,—like Mrs. Raikes' carpet. I don't see why she's to have a prettier carpet than us, now we've got five thousand pounds."

"We haven't got it yet, Sue," says grannie.

"Well, we're going to have it," mother answered. "And we may just as well get the carpet. I don't see why we should wait."

"Nor I neither," father said.

"I do," said grannie, looking at them. "Miles, if you take my advice, you'll do nothing in a hurry."

But father was in no mood for waiting, nor mother either. The new carpet was chosen, and a grand one we children thought it, for there were huge bunches of red and purple flowers and green leaves, on a sort of yellowish ground. The old carpet, which had lasted nearly all through grannie's married life until now, was a real Brussels, and it had only a small brown pattern with a little red in it. The new was not a Brussels, but only a cheap sort of tapestry, which Mr. Trowgood said would wear "next door to a Brussels." And the bunches of flowers were so big, that only four whole ones could get into our little bit of a parlour. And the odd part of the matter was, that the room seemed all at once to have grown much smaller. I didn't know why then, though I am sure now that it was because the pattern was too large for the size of the room. Small-patterned carpets and papers always make a room seem bigger. When I asked grannie how she liked it, she only said: "I love the dear old carpet, Phœbe. No new one can ever be what the old one was to me."

Four new chairs with stuffed blue seats and yellow buttons were bought at the same time; and they did smarten up the room wonderfully, there's no denying. The new sofa was blue too, only it did not quite match the chairs. And the clock looked grand on the mantel-shelf, for it had a lot of gilt about it. It went all right for two days, and then it stopped, and wouldn't go any longer. But when father spoke about it, Trowgood said it must have been wrongly wound up, and father was so afraid of vexing him that he didn't complain any more.

Mother got herself the new cap, and a fine new bonnet too, and she spent a good deal of time before the looking-glass, trying them on. And the only thing grannie said about it all to me was: "They must learn, Phœbe. People have to learn by experience. You and I can't help it. Maybe all will come right in the end. But if you want to please me, my dear, you'll not wear the coral necklace yet awhile."

"No, I won't, grannie," I said. "I'll wait till you put on your new gown."

C H A P T E R V I

An Alarm

A FEW days later, father suddenly found that all was not quite so sure as he had thought about the five thousand pounds. For the son, who had expected the money, made up his mind to "dispute the will," as it is called. He went to the lawyers, and tried to prove that it was all a mistake, and that the money ought properly to go to him, not us. He wanted to make out that his old father had not been right in the head, at the time that he made the will. If he could show this to be the case, it would of course make all the difference.

I shall never forget seeing father come in, just after hearing that the will was to be disputed. It was Saturday morning, and we were going to have the Jenkinses and the Dickensons and the Raikes' to dinner, and afterwards there was to be an excursion of all of us together to a place called Sunny Point, where we were going to have a sort of picnic tea in some respectable tea-gardens.

There had been quite a struggle, because father was bent on a Sunday dinner to the neighbours, and grannie was set against it. Father was downright angry, and mother cried and fretted because grannie would not give in. Grannie did not say very much, for it wasn't her way to waste words; but she did say she would have nothing to do with the matter, for she couldn't on principle make God's day one of junketing and pleasure. But nothing could be done without her; for mother was a poor cook, and the dinner would just have been a failure altogether, if grannie had not cooked it. Then, when father was vexed and mother upset, grannie quietly asked why it could not be Saturday instead, and offered to do anything they liked for Saturday. And so it was settled.

Grannie and I had been hard at work, for I always helped her, and we had a beautiful dinner nearly ready. Grannie did not like the expense of it all; but having made a stand about the more important matter of Sabbath-breaking, she would not make a stir about this too. So there was to be for once a thorough good turn-out. Grannie had her Sunday dress ready to put on at the last moment, and I had put on mine already, and mother was in the parlour, wearing her new green silk, with bright glass buttons all down the front, and a cap with pink bows. She did look smart, and no mistake; and the blue sofa and chairs and the gay carpet helped to make her still smarter. I peeped in once or twice in the middle of my work, and saw her fidgeting about and making a grand rustling. But somehow it didn't seem like mother. I'd rather have had her as I was used.

Then I was back in the kitchen with grannie: and I was just lifting off a saucepan from the fire when I heard a shriek. It startled me so, that I very nearly dropped the saucepan; and well scalded I should have been if I had.

"Steady, Phœbe," grannie said. "One thing at a time, my dear. Put that down safely. Now go and ask what is the matter. I saw your father come in."

I rushed off to the parlour, and found mother in tears, with her face as red as fire. But father was the worst. I never saw father look so before. The first thought that came into my mind was that a wicked spirit must have got inside him. And though I tried to put the thought away, it came back. Father was talking fast

in a loud fierce tone, and it made me tremble. I heard him use
a bad word, and that frightened me, for I had never heard him
say bad words. Grannie was so particular, and she had brought
him up to be the same. He may have been different among other
people; but before grannie and with us children, he had always
been careful. I suppose he was in such a passion that he hardly
knew what he was saying. And I just rushed back to the kitchen,
and dragged grannie with me to the parlour.

"What is the matter?" said she, looking at them.

"Matter!" father said, and he turned round upon her, and said
the words again, in a fierce sort of way. Grannie went up to him
and put her hand on his shoulder.

"Miles," she said, "you never spoke so before me yet, and you
won't again, if you don't want to break your old mother's heart."

"A man can't be always choosing his words," father said roughly,
and he shook her hand off. "Here's a nice go! That fellow's setting
to work to prove that the old man was mad when he made the will."

"I expected as much," grannie said. "And if they prove it?"

"They can't prove it. I'd defy all England to prove it,—without
a pack of lies is to be taken as truth," father said in a passionate
way. "The old man was as clear in the head as you or I."

Grannie didn't ask him how he knew this, since he had not
seen Andrew Morison for years. She only said: "But if they do
prove it?"

"They can't, I tell you. If they did, the money wouldn't come
to us. But they can't-they shan't!" And father stamped his foot.

"The money is left to us, and it's ours. It's ours!"

"Maybe it'll be ours by-and-by," grannie said. "I hope it may
be, if it's for our good. But it isn't ours yet, Miles, and I should
be better satisfied, for my part, if you had waited, and not got all
these things."

"I shouldn't," father shouted, seeming as if he wanted to
drown everybody's speech except his own. "I shouldn't be better

satisfied; and what's more, I shan't stop. The money's sure to come. Old Morison was as clear-headed as yourself, mother, and if there's any right and justice in the land, they'll give it so. It's like Jem Morison's sneaking ways to go and do this. But he'll fail. He'll fail, as sure as my name is Miles Murdock. I hope they'll saddle him with costs too, and serve him out."

"Somebody has to be disappointed, anyway," grannie said. "And it's worse for him than for you: for he's been expecting for years, and you've only thought about it a little while. But the meat'll be spoiling, if I don't go and see to it."

"And, oh dear me! there's the Dickensons coming, and it's half-past twelve, and I've got such a red face," mother said. "O dear me! I wish you hadn't gone and told us until they were gone. What shall we do, if the money don't come after all? You don't really think we shan't have it, do you, Miles?"

"No, I don't," father said shortly; but it was plain he didn't feel easy in his mind.

Grannie and I went back to the kitchen, and she did not abate one jot of care for all that had to be done; but presently she gave a sigh, and said to herself,—"How ever in the world folks can be so silly!"

"Father and mother?" I asked.

"I didn't mean that for you, Phœbe," said she. "It's no place of a child to blame her parents. But it is a want of sense. Supposing the money don't come after all?"

"Wouldn't you be very sorry?" I asked.

"Maybe so," she said. "Five thousand pounds has a tempting sound, and I like things to be easy and plentiful as well as others do. But I do say, and I mean it too, that I'd sooner it should never come at all, than have you all go wrong with its coming."

"But why should we, grannie?" I asked. "Why should we? Lots of folks have money, as much as that and more, and don't go wrong with it."

"True enough," she said. "But it's the sudden riches after being poor that's the danger, Phœbe. It isn't the keeping on with what one's used to. There's many a head been turned, and many a heart gone wrong, with sudden riches. I don't say but what there's grace enough to keep one through the danger, if we'll seek it—if we'll ask it, Phœbe."

And I knew she meant that father and mother were not thinking of danger, and were not asking to be kept through it.

Dinner had soon to be dished up and taken in. Grannie changed her dress in a hurry, for father would not have been happy without. The Dickensons and all the rest were come, and our little parlour was just stuffed full. I saw the neighbours eyeing mother's green silk; and one or two of them made faces at one another about it on the sly, and I thought they were jealous. But they need not have been, if they had known how we were thinking about that silk dress, supposing the money should not come! Mrs. Dickenson asked mother where she had got it; and Mrs. Jenkins wanted to know how much she had paid by the yard; and Mrs. Raikes fingered it and said she knew of better to be had at a less price. And I did not think all this was quite mannerly, somehow; but mother seemed to like it, and she became quite merry.

But father had a gloomy look, and I saw that he could not forget what he had heard. Just as we were sitting down to dinner, he spied me and said—

"Where is your necklace, Phœbe?"

"I didn't put it on, father," I said, getting red in the face.

"Then go and put it on this minute, Phœbe," he said angrily.

I could not help trembling a little, and I only just managed to get out the words,—"Grannie said—"

"I don't care what grannie said, nor anybody else neither. Go and put it on,—d'you hear?"

I looked at grannie, and she said, "Do as father tells you, Phœbe."

So I rushed off, and put it on. But I did not like doing so. I had a sort of feeling that it was bought with money which was not ours, and which never might be, and I seemed almost to hate the coral necklace. For I could not bear to see grannie sad, and father so unlike himself.

I don't think any of us enjoyed that Saturday very much, though to be sure there was plenty of talk and of laughing.

C H A P T E R   V I I

To Go or to Stay

THOUGH father had said he did not mean to stop getting things from Trowgood's, because he was so sure the money would come to us, still he thought better of this. I am not at all sure that Trowgood, hearing what was going on, did not give father a hint that it was best to wait. Anyway we did wait.

I think this waiting-time was a good thing for us. At least, I know it was good for me; and I suppose it might have been good for the others too, if they had been willing. For of course one must be willing, before anything can do one good in life; and father and mother were not willing. Father never seemed to think of any part of the matter as coming straight from God. All he talked about was Jem Morison and the lawyers—and very hotly he did talk at times.

But, as I say, the waiting was good, or it ought to have been goad. It gave us leisure for thought, and for getting over the first excitement of the news. It's well to be able to sift and weigh a matter, before having to take action. To be sure, father had acted already, as regarded the things bought; but still in some measure his hands had been tied, and now they were tied yet more.

One Sunday afternoon grannie and I were sitting together, having our tea. The other three had been to dinner with the Raikes', and were not back yet: so we were afraid there must be some sort of Sunday excursion as well as dinner. Grannie and I had been having a nice quiet afternoon together, and grannie seemed tired, so I got the tea for her earlier than usual, and we had the kettle boiling in good time.

"If they don't come soon, they won't be in time for Church," I said.

"Not for the first time," grannie answered, and she spoke in a sad sort of way. "I'm sore afraid of its being a habit that will grow. It's wonderful how anything of a bad habit does grow. Just let it alone like a weed, and it's sure to sprout. I suppose good habits go against the grain, for they do take a deal of tending."

"But father was brought up to Church-going," I said.

"Yes, yes, he was brought up to it. There wasn't anything a-wanting in the bringing-up, so far as I know. But though a mother's bringing-up can do a lot, it can't put God's grace into a man's heart. It can't do that."

"Father always used to like so much to go to Church," I said.

"He liked to please his old mother, Phœbe," said she. "That's what it was—not so much of liking the worship of God for its own sake. I'd sooner it had been that—more hope of its lasting, if it had. But the pleasing of his old mother isn't so much to him now. He's got little thought or care save for his five thousand pounds—which mayn't ever be his really neither."

"Do you think it won't come to us, grannie?" I asked, and I couldn't help longing that it might.

"I don't think either way," said she. "It may or it mayn't. I've no manner of means of knowing whether Andrew Morison was in his right senses or no. If it does come it'll be a solemn trust from God; and I'm sorely afraid lest it should be squandered away with no thought at all of Him in the spending."

"Mother was talking again yesterday about going into a bigger house," I said. "She does want it so, grannie; and father is quite set on five hundred a year, and not only two hundred."

"Well, you nor I can't check him," she said. "But this cottage is mine, and it shan't be sold while I live. If they go, I'll stay on here and work for myself. It's little I should want. I'm too old for settling into a new home at my time of life. I've been thirty years and more here, and please God I'll stay till I die."

"O grannie! I hope if they go they'll let me live with you," I said.

"No," she answered, "that isn't likely. They'll want you to work for them—without they're going to set up grand, and have servants like gentlefolks. I'd believe in pretty near any sort of folly. But, there—I'm forgetting—that's no sort of manner to speak in to you about them. You're but a child, and you've got to do as you are told."

"But if we live in another house away from you—and if they tell me to do things that are wrong! O grannie! do come with us," I cried; and I turned and caught hold of her dress, and held it fast. "It's only you that can keep us straight."

"Only me!" said she.

And she sat looking before her, not at me but at something which I could not see, as it were, and a sort of glow came into her face, as it was wont to do, once in a way. And I cried again, holding her tightly still, "O grannie! don't let us be apart. Everything will go wrong in the new house, if you won't come there with us."

"You're right and you're wrong, Phœbe," she said at last, arousing herself and fixing her eyes upon me. "You're wrong and you're right. Yes—wrong. For it isn't I that can keep you straight— you nor any of them. I,—why I can't keep myself, much less other folks! It's God that can keep you straight, and none other."

Then, after a little pause, she went on—

"But you're right too, and I see it now. I can't keep you right, but maybe God would use me. It's little enough I could do; but what if He wants me to do that little? Yes—I see now. I've been clinging in thought to the old home—and I do cling, and I love the very walls and boards; and a new home at my time of life would be nigh a heart-break to me, after all the years and years I've lived here, first with your grandfather, and then with your father. But

I've been forgetting to ask what was the right thing for me to do. It isn't sense for me to cling more to boards and rafters than to living flesh and blood. And after all, you'll need me more than the old home will. It's a dear old home to me, Phœbe. But love may be selfish, and I think mine has been so. I'll have to keep stricter watch for the future. And if you all go, I'll come too. Maybe it'll not be for long—that's as God wills. But I'll not leave you to fight on alone, till God calls me—and then I'll have no choice, and I'll be content to leave the rest to Him. So we'll go all together, Phœbe. Will that set your mind at rest, child?"

"O grannie! it's all I wanted," I said. "Everything's sure to go straight now."

But she shook her head and said, "It's the old old story,— leaning on a broken reed. I suppose it isn't till the reed gives way under us, that we turn to lean on God."

The New House

IT was only two or three days after that Sunday afternoon, that we heard of the money being sure to us. The matter had been gone into, and James Morison had done his very best to prove that his old father was crazed at the time of the making of the will. I dare say he believed it himself, after a fashion. Most people can manage to believe a thing, if they want it very much to be true. But there was no real proof, and his case broke down. A good many people were ready to say what a shame it was of the old man to disinherit his son; but none had power to undo the deed done.

"So now it's quite certain—certain and sure," father said. "No more need to croak and look dismal, mother. Now the money's ours, and we'll do our best to get a little pleasure out of it."

Grannie had been looking grave, but not dismal, for it wasn't her way. Some people call everything dismal that isn't full of noisy merriment. I never could see, for my part, why one should be the happier for making a noise. Grannie did not seem put out, though, at his words. She only looked up at him, and said—"No, Miles, the money is not yours."

"Well, well, it soon will be," said he, "if you must be so particular."

"No," said she in the same manner. "It never will be yours, my dear."

"Why, grannie, what silly notion have you got in your head now?" said he quite angrily. "Never will be mine! I tell you, the thing is as sure and certain as can be, and the money's as good as mine already. The matter's settled, and Jem Morison is beat out-and-out. It'll come, sure enough."

"Yes, maybe," she answered. "The five thousand pounds is coming to you, Miles, my dear; but it's only lent. It isn't yours. 'The silver and gold are the Lord's.' He only lends it, Miles."

"Oh, of course—to be sure," father said, his face clearing. "I didn't see what you were at. That's all right and well, mother—and quite proper for one at your age to be religious. But it don't alter the fact that I'm to have five thousand pounds."

"Yes, to have it in your hands," grannie said. "But there'll be a day of reckoning, Miles, and every penny of that you'll have to account for to Him who owns it. I've thought it sometimes a fearful thing for rich folks, with their thousands and thousands, lent them by God to be spent for Him, and all to be accounted for. And now we'll have some of that same burden to bear."

"One would think we were going in for some awful trouble, only to hear you speak," father said. "But you're not going to put me into the dismals, mother, for all you can say. If it's a burden, it's an uncommon pleasant sort. Wish it was a little heavier, that's all."

"Yes, that's the way with men," says grannie quietly. "You'll soon begin to look on five thousand pounds as nothing, and to wish it was ten."

"Well, I shouldn't mind now, if it was ten," father said.

The next thing that came up was about a change of house. Mother wouldn't let the matter rest. Father did not seem to like the thought at first, for he knew how grannie was set against it. Grannie did not say to them what she had said to me, but just waited; and I did not tell it either. But mother let father have no peace. She was bent on getting a house in the same row with the

Raikes', and on having a parlour that would beat Mrs. Raikes' parlour in smartness.

She and father talked it over one day, when grannie was not at hand. Father said he knew grannie would never leave the cottage; and mother said, it did not matter, for we should be quite near. Father said, it did matter, for there would be nothing straight without her, and nobody to do the work and the cooking, "and Phœbe couldn't manage all that alone." Mother said, "No, of course not, but we would keep a girl like the Raikes', and manage so." Father said he didn't see who would cook. And mother said, "Phœbe would, of course." Father said he didn't see why I was to drudge while others took their ease; but it was no good talking, for if grannie wouldn't come too, he should not leave the cottage. Mother pouted, and said that father cared more for grannie than for her. Father said it wasn't true; and mother said, yes, it was, or he wouldn't want her to live in a horrid little pokey hole, when he could afford her a nice house as well as not. And then she cried, and talked about her own home, when she was a girl, and wished she had never left it. Mother's father had been a tallow-chandler, and well-to-do, and mother had been a spoilt child.

Just when they got so far, grannie walked in. She heard mother's last words, and asked what it all meant. Father told her, and she said—"What's your wish, Miles?"

"I don't want to go without you, mother," says he. "I've never lived apart from you yet, and I don't mean to, if I can help it. I should think of you as lonesome here; and we should want you too."

"But that's your only reason?" says she. "You've no feeling at leaving the old place."

"Well, no—can't say as I have," said father. "I shouldn't mind a scrap more room to turn round in."

"And the money?" said she.

"Oh, that's all right," says he. "I'm going to invest, so as it'll bring us in nigh upon five hundred a year."

"Mr. Scott didn't count so much to be safe."

"Mr. Scott don't know everything," father said. "I suppose I'm as good a judge as most. I'm not going to throw the money away, mother, you may be sure. But supposing we say four hundred a year,—it don't make so much difference. We can afford a bigger house than this, anyway."

"Well, you must do what you think best," grannie said. "You're not a boy now, to take an old woman's advice. A man must look out for himself. I'll leave you to settle about the other house, Miles. It don't so much matter to me. I'm an old woman, and I can't look to live in any house many more years. I did say at first that I never would of my own free will go out of this, where I've been all my married life. But maybe that was selfishness. Maybe I could be of more use going than staying. If it's God's will for me, I'm willing— that's all. So you needn't think about me, Miles. If you both feel it's the best and right thing to do, I'll come with you."

Father seemed very pleased. I had not seen him so kind for a good while past. He said more than once—"That's right, mother—things'll go straight now."

The very next day father came in, saying there was a house to let in Pleasant Row, only three doors off from the Raikes'. I wondered if mother had seen it before. She and father went to look it over, and when they came back they could talk of nothing else. The rent was forty pounds, and that seemed a deal; but mother said—"What was forty pounds out of five hundred?" It was only a small house, but the rents in the town had been getting very high of late.

The house had to be taken at once, if at all, for somebody else was asking after it. Grannie begged father to wait and do nothing till the money should come. But he said it would be a thousand pities to miss the chance, for they might not find another so nice, and he could easily get the money lent him for the first quarter's rent.

"We needn't move in yet, you know," he said.

So it was all settled, and the next thing spoken about was that the cottage must be sold. I think that did go to grannie's heart. But she never made a word of complaint—only sometimes I saw her looking at one thing and another, as if she were saying such a sorrowful good-bye. Poor grannie! I wondered often at her patience.

CHAPTER IX
Nothing to Do

TROWGOOD was willing to trust to any amount for the furniture; so the making ready of the new house began at once. Mother said she did not see any good in waiting, for the bills could be paid as soon as ever the money came, and father was of the same mind.

There was a great deal to be done to the house. Father took it in such a hurry, that he did not have a proper agreement made; and when he found afterwards what a number of repairs were wanted, he had to do it all himself, for the landlord was a churlish sort of body, and said "No" to pretty nearly everything asked.

Mother was vexed because father had not thought of these matters sooner; but father said, what did it signify? He seemed to think five thousand pounds could do everything.

He and mother were agreed on one head, and that was that the house must make a smart appearance. The top rooms were damp, and the kitchen had water oozing out all over the walls, and there was a queer sort of smell in the parlour, which grannie said ought to be attended to. She said our cottage had always been so sweet and dry, and that was partly how we had all kept such good health. She told father he had a deal better have the dampness and the smell cured, and spend less on carpets and gimcracks. But mother said—"Who cared for a little wet?" and father said,—"All in good time, grannie." And he seemed to think the "good time" should come late, not early.

The new carpet, which was chosen in such a hurry for our cottage, would not fit the new parlour, and Trowgood said he could not get any more of the same pattern. Mother seemed rather glad. She had that put into the biggest bedroom,—at least she settled that it should go there when we moved,—and she chose another, quite as smart, which cost a great deal more, and so she liked it better.

It is wonderful what a number of things are wanted in a new house. Mother did not seem to care to keep anything out of the dear old cottage. Grannie and I were to sleep together still, and we settled to furnish our room with things that we had by us, and to have nothing new at all. But whatever we did not want for our room was to be sold. Mother seemed bent on having all quite fresh. I think the thought of parting with the old furniture that she loved so much cut very deeply with grannie.

Father was still working for the Johnstones, but he did not work regular as he was used to do before. He seemed to have a sort of distaste for it. Sundays were getting to be just days of pleasure and amusement, with no thought of God in them; and on Monday he commonly had a lazy fit, and lounged about doing nothing. Sometimes the lazy fit lasted over Tuesday as well. He used before to have a bright brisk way of doing things, but he was losing that now. I think Mr. Johnstone or the foreman must have found fault with him once or twice, for I heard him talking about them angrily, and saying "he wouldn't be driven—not he,—thank goodness he had enough and to spare now, and he should please himself."

I don't at all know whether father meant to go on with the same work, after he got his money. I think it is likely he was in a sort of uncertain state, waiting to see what to do. He would have money enough to start him in something better, or even to live an idle life. But he had been trained to no other kind of work; and it is quite certain that no hale and hearty man in middle life can be happy with nothing to do. There are men who can make their own work and find their own interests,—men who can be quite happy in doing good to others, or in studying God's works, or in reading books. But reading was always a labour to father, and he knew and cared nothing about study; and I don't suppose he ever thought of such a thing as steady doing of good to others, though of course he would have been ready any day to give a crust to a starving man, if he came across him by chance.

But, as I say, I do not know what father really meant to do. I think it startled him, and I am sure it was a great shock to us all, when Mr. Johnstone dismissed him from his employ.

There was no warning given; except that I believe there had been several complaints of father's irregular way of working. Mr. Johnstone did not speak to father himself. The foreman told him he would not be wanted any more, after a certain day. Father was angry and wanted to know why. The answer was, that Mr. Johnstone had not been satisfied with him for a good while, and as he had rather more hands than he wanted just then, of course those who had been least steady at work must be the first to go.

Years later I heard more, in other quarters. I know now that poor father had more than once forgotten himself, and had spoken in an uppish sort of way, and had talked too much of his "good luck," and had seemed to think himself pretty much on a level with his master. And neither master nor men liked it. I know that Mr. Johnstone told a friend he found father's influence "demoralising," whatever that might mean. He said the other men were getting unsettled and discontented, and he could not allow it to go on.

But we had known nothing of all this; and when father came home, and told us he was not to work there any more, we did not know what to think of it.

Father was very angry, and yet he tried to seem as if he did not care. He talked big, and said he was right glad, and he didn't mean to be any more at the beck and call of that fellow Sykes. Sykes was the foreman. Mother seemed half frightened and half pleased.

And grannie was very quiet, and her dear face looked so pale. I had seen that pale look often lately, and I knew she was fretted and worried. She said at last,—"What are you going to do, Miles?"

"Do! Why, stay away," says he roughly.

"But the money isn't come yet, and we can't live on nothing till it does," grannie said.

"Oh, there's no need," father said. "I could get other work easy enough. But I don't see why I'm to work like a poor man, when I have five thousand pounds of my own. I don't see it at all."

"God's law is work," said grannie in a low voice. "He gave us the Sunday for rest. But He gave us a clear command too,—'SIX DAYS SHALT THOU LABOUR.'"

"It's a command lots of people break, then," said father.

I think that father, like a good many people, fancied "work" and "labour" can only mean bodily toil. I know better now. I have seen more of life, and I know there are many different kinds of work,—hand-work, and head-work, and heart-work. The man that is piling up bricks and mortar may not be toiling one quarter so hard, as the man who sits quiet in a chair, working out some deep thought for other men, or the woman who wears herself out in ceaseless watching of her children and caring for their good.

"What are we to do, Miles?" grannie asked again.

"Oh, I'll see about it," said father. "There's no hurry. I'll get a job or two somewhere. And they'll let us have things on credit anywhere. My good fortune is well enough known. We shan't starve."

"Maybe not," grannie said. "But if you don't look out, my dear, you'll make a big hole in your five thousand pounds, before ever it comes to you."

Father laughed loud at the idea. The money seemed to him too much ever to come to an end. Grannie went out of the room, and I went after her, I didn't know why. She crossed into the parlour, and sat down, and I was frightened at the look in her face.

"It's nothing," she said,—"only a sort of fainty feeling that comes over me once in a while. Just to show me I'm an old woman, maybe. Don't you mind."

"O grannie, is it because you're fretting at having to leave the old home?" I asked: for I knew how it grieved her.

"I dare say it is," she said: "I've a silly sort of fondness for places, and somehow I've never felt right and like myself since that was settled. But I'll have no words spoken to them, Phœbe. For it's not that which cuts most deep. It is seeing how things are tending, and knowing I can do nought to stop what is wrong."

And I knew what she meant.

C H A P T E R   X

Mr. Simmons

ABOUT ten days after this, father said to us one morning that we were to have a nice dinner ready, for he was going to bring home a friend with him. He would not tell us who it was. "Nobody you know," he said. So we did as we were told, and asked no questions.

The friend was one that we had never seen before. He was a little bit of a man, with a soft smooth manner of speaking, and grey eyes that had a sharp trick of seeing everything and yet that never looked anybody straight in the face. He had a smart ring on his little finger, and studs that looked like big diamonds. Mother thought him "quite a gentleman," and was as proud as could be to have him at her table. But grannie laughed when mother called him so; for grannie had been in good service when she was young, and she knew well enough the difference between a gentleman and not a gentleman.

However, it was plain that Mr. Simmons thought himself a grand person, and counted it a condescension to dine in our cottage. He and father seemed to know a deal about one another that nobody else knew. I didn't like the way he nodded and winked at some things that were said between them. And I liked still less the sort of sneer that came over his face, when grannie once made mention of the Bible.

After dinner father went off with Mr. Simmons, and did not come back till late. When he did, he pulled out his purse and said, "It's all right," and handed mother a five-pound note.

"Has the money come?" asked mother. She was always asking that question.

"No, but it won't be long," father said. "And I've a friend now, willing to advance whatever we need till it does come."

"What makes him willing to do that, Miles?" says grannie, quite sharp-like.

"Why, just in a friendly way," said father.

"Is it only in a friendly way?" says grannie. "That's odd, when he don't know us, and has no particular call to do the kindness. Do you mean to say he don't look to turn a penny by it?"

"Oh, well,—of course there's the interest," father said carelessly. "A man couldn't be expected to put himself to inconvenience for nothing at all."

"How much is the interest?" asked grannie.

"Well, he did speak of fifteen or twenty per cent for small sums, but that was before we got so friendly together. I don't doubt but he'll make it lower now. You needn't fidget, grannie. It's a mere song, just a few pounds and odd shillings."

Grannie waited a minute or two, thinking to herself, and then she said in a slow sort of way—

"Miles, Mr. Simmons is a bad man."

"Now mother!" said he.

"Mr. Simmons is a bad man," repeated grannie, "and you may take my word for it."

"That's charity, isn't it?" said father. "A man you've never seen in your life before, and one as is just doing me a good turn."

"I don't want to be uncharitable," grannie said. "But I know a bad man when I see him, and he's one. And he'll get you into trouble, as sure as you have to do with him."

"I'm not a boy to be lectured, mother," says he very short. "I hope I'm of an age to choose my own friends, and not be meddled with. I can tell you Simmons is a clever fellow and no mistake. Dear me, I don't know what there is he don't know."

"That may be," grannie said. "But cleverness isn't goodness. I wish it was. The world would be a better world than it is."

And then she dropped the subject, and said no more. That was always her way. She spoke out where she counted it right, but she didn't go on bothering where her words had no power.

Mother was so pleased to have her five-pound note, that she seemed to care very little for what was being said. She went off that same afternoon, and got some new roses for her bonnet, and a smart ribbon, and a big brooch. Father laughed when he saw them, and said he had meant the money for the butcher and baker and milkman, for we had been having things on credit since he left off work; but he went on to add that it didn't matter, for there was plenty more. And next day he brought another five-pound note, and gave it to grannie, and told mother to do what she liked with the other. Every penny of it went in dress. Grannie said to herself, "It's a sort of madness;" but I do not think she meant me to hear.

Another three or four months went by, and still the money did not come. More five-pound notes followed the first, and money had to be borrowed fur the rent of the new house, as well as for our every-day expenses. Mother said one day that she could not see why we should not go into it straight off, and get rid of the old cottage. What was the good of waiting? she asked. It would not cost us much more to live in the house than in the cottage. Perhaps there was some truth in this as we were now living; for father was getting to be very particular about having the best of everything at table; and he and mother seemed quite careless how many bills they ran up.

Grannie said nothing, only she went very white again. But father took up the notion at once. He said it was folly to be keeping up two homes, and the quicker we moved the better. So the bills were run up higher still, in getting lots of new things to make the other house quite ready; for mother was set on having all "genteel," as she said. It was settled that we were to get in before Christmas Day, and father began trying to find somebody to buy the cottage.

Grannie was very loth to have the cottage sold. She stood out for awhile, and it could not be done without her consent. She wanted it to be only let; so that it might be ours still, if we ever wanted it again. But father was very much vexed, for he wanted the ready money; and he told her she always thwarted him in everything, and he threatened to go and borrow a hundred pounds right away from Mr. Simmons. Grannie gave in at last, but how she did cry! I think she and I both hoped father would not succeed. But he did, for there was a run upon the place in those days; and he was in such a hurry to get the matter settled, that he was willing to take less than the real value of the cottage, on condition that he should have quick payment. It was not long before he came in and told us that the thing was done.

"Grannie, are you very sorry?" I asked of her that night, when we were up in our little room, and she sat down in a sort of tired-out way on the foot of the bed.

"Mayhap I shouldn't be," she said. "It's no real harm for me to have my heart pulled loose from this world, and set on things higher." And she began to murmur, in a sort of half-singing voice, which quavered a little—

"'My rest is in heaven, my rest is not here;
Then why should I murmur when trials are near?
Be hushed, my dark spirit, the worst that can come
But shortens thy journey, and hastens thee home.'"

"O don't, please, grannie," I said. "I don't want you to think of that."

"I'm always thinking of it," she said. "That's my only home now, Phœbe. I've no home again in this world. You young things can take to fresh places easy enough, and it's only right. But I can't. I'm like an old tree pulled up by the roots. It'll never take kindly to another soil. I think uprooting means dying in such a case. Not that

I'm murmuring, my dear. One must have trouble. And if it wasn't for the change in Miles, I could stand other things easier."

"You aren't so very old, grannie," I said. "I wish you wouldn't talk about dying, please. You work ever so much harder than mother does. And we'll all be together, and I'll be such a good girl, and I think we shall be happy. Don't you think so? Won't you try, grannie?" And I know I looked at her in a beseeching sort of way.

"O yes, I'll try," said she. "I don't doubt but what I'll be happy. I couldn't be aught else, with the thought of God loving and caring for me. But it won't be home, Phœbe, my dear."

And I knew she spoke truth, though I tried not to think it.

C H A P T E R X I

Going Home

THE evening came which was to have been our last in the old home, for the very next day we were to have left it—just one week before Christmas Day.

It was bitterly cold weather, and grannie seemed to shrink under the cold, as she had not been used to do. The other house was all furnished and ready, except just the room for grannie and me, and that was to have its furniture taken from the cottage on the morrow. Everything left behind would be sold.

I didn't think the cottage had ever seemed more snug and home-like than on that day. Snow lay thick on the roof and in the little garden, but all inside was so cosy. I could not believe we were really going.

Grannie seemed to have upon her a strange dread of the new home, a strange shrinking from it, as if she were leaving a warm nest, and going out into the cold and damp. I could not talk her out of the feeling. She said it was silly, she knew, and she could not account for it, but she had the dread. And many times that day she said sorrowfully—"It won't be home, Phœbe. I've no home now on earth. I didn't think I should ever have to leave the old place." And then she would add—"But it is God's will, and I mustn't grumble. What does it matter? There's a better Home above."

She was very tired in the evening, with a sort of pinched blue look in her face, which I hadn't ever seen there before. Father noticed it, and he said she had done too much, and he made her sit in the arm-chair, and was quite nice and kind to her. I think she found that a comfort. Mother was rushing about everywhere, making believe to be busy, though really not doing much, for there was not much to be done. Grannie had put everything into beautiful order for the move.

"Miles," grannie said, all of a sudden—"I'm wondering if you'll do something to please your old mother."

"To be sure I will," said he, for he was in great good humour that day. "What is it? Something new you want? Sue buys lots of things, and you don't spend a penny on yourself."

"I've enough and to spare," she said. "I'll wait till the pennies come before I spend 'em, my dear. No need for more borrowing and buying than goes on already. I hope it isn't all a mistake, Miles."

"Mistake!—no," says he. "There's no mistake about the five thousand pounds. That's sure enough."

"So you may think—so you and me may think," said she, in a dreamy sort of way. "But who knows? Riches take wings and fly away."

"Mine shan't," father said. "I'll take right good care to hold my own fast. Money don't fly away if it isn't thrown away, I take it. But what did you want me to get for you?"

"It wasn't anything I wanted you to get," she said.

"Because I don't mind what it is," said he. "I can afford it, you know. Only I'd have you use what I get, not lay it by like that black dress, you know."

"Ah—that dress," says she softly. "I'm glad it's black. Yes, it'll do—for Sue."

Father stared, and she gave him a little smile.

"I was only a-thinking," she said. "But the thing I want you to do isn't buying, Miles. You haven't been often to Church of late, and it's getting seldomer and seldomer. Will you promise me to go regular when we get into the new home?"

"Why—I am regular," says he. "I don't stay away without there's good reason."

"Reason maybe, but not good reason," says she. "Pleasuring's no good reason for leaving the worship of God. You said you'd do what I was going to ask you, Miles."

"O well—yes—we'll see," said he. "I didn't know what it was."

"But now you do know," she said, "you're not going to say 'No' to me?"

"We'll see," was all he would answer.

"I'm going to bed early," she said. "I feel out of sorts somehow, and I've a queer sort of weakness on me. But it's our last night in the old home. I should like to finish off the life here with Bible-reading and prayer. It's an old woman's fancy you'll say, Miles, but I should."

"What for?" asked mother, who had come in and was listening.

"It's fitting," grannie said. "God's blessing has been on us here, and He has cared for us; and we'd ought to thank Him, and ask for the same in the new home too."

"Well, I'm busy just now," mother said, and she went off quick and didn't come back.

But father got up, and brought the big Bible to grannie. "I'm not religious like you, mother," he said; "but you shall have your will—if it's a pleasure. Only it's you that must do it, not I."

She didn't press him for more. She just turned over the leaves, and found the 103rd Psalm, and read it aloud. And I couldn't help noticing how her dear face grew bright, with a sort of inward glow, as if God Himself was speaking to her heart.

"It's full of mercy and loving-kindness—full—full," she said at the end. "Miles, I'd give anything—"

"What for, mother?" said he, and his voice was husky.

"If you'd be willing to have God for such a Friend as He's been to me," said she.

And then she made us kneel down—father and Asaph and me, and she prayed. How she did pray, thanking God, and asking Him to keep us from dangers, and speaking the Name of Jesus so lovingly, and seeming just as if she had Someone just close beside her, listening! And hadn't she?

But all at once she stopped, and then went on, and stopped again, and seemed confused. And then she said "Phœbe." And the next moment she fell down heavily, all in a heap, with no life in her, as it were.

Father carried her upstairs, and put her on her bed; and mother cried and was frightened. And all we could do, she would not come to herself. At first we only thought she was knocked up and faint, but presently we began to see that things were worse, and father went off for the doctor.

When the doctor came, he said grannie was very ill indeed, and could not possibly be moved next day. He said it must have been coming on for some days, and he told us pretty plainly that he did not believe she would get over it. "She's an old woman, you know," he said.

I did not half know what he meant. It seemed too dreadful to think of grannie dying. I never knew till then how much I loved her.

I had a busy enough life the next week, what with nursing and work. I couldn't bear to leave grannie, yet mother expected me to do all that I commonly did and attend to grannie too. Our move had to be put off, of course, and mother was vexed. She did not believe that grannie was so bad as the doctor said. Father was very anxious, and he stayed a great deal at home, and often sat with grannie. But she did not know him or any of us.

Things went on so up to Christmas Eve. And then there was just a little glimmer of sense. She seemed to look at me, and I heard her say, "Home! going Home!"

"Perhaps not just yet, grannie," I said. But she smiled again, in a sort of eager way. She had pretty nearly lost the power of speech, yet she managed to say again, "Going Home—Home, Phœbe."

And that was all. She looked peaceful, and we thought her better. Mr. Scott came to see her a little later, but she had dropped into a sleep, and from that sleep she never woke. Nobody could tell the moment when she died, she went so quietly.

It was a sad Christmas for us all, and saddest of all, I think, for me; for I had been more her child than mother's, and she had taught me everything, and I seemed to feel as if I didn't know how to live without her.

Father was miserable, for he had loved her dearly. It was only of late that he had ever said a sharp word to her, and I suppose those sharp words came back now and troubled him. And he had no real comfort like me; so after all he was the worst off. For I could think of grannie in her happy Home, with the Lord Jesus and the bright angels, singing songs to God; but father could only think about his own loss. He did not care to think about Heaven, and he only felt very wretched. And the day after grannie's death, he did what he had never never done before—stayed ever so long at the public-house drinking, and came back the worse for what he had taken.

C H A P T E R XII

At Last

THE day before the New Year grannie's body was laid to rest in the green churchyard. But grannie herself was not there. I used to think of how she was singing, away in her heavenly home, and that was the only comfort I had in my great sorrow.

The next day we went into our other house, to begin our new life. And a new life indeed it was without grannie, much more new on that account than because we had a fresh roof over our heads.

Father seemed greatly ashamed of himself, for having gone to the public-house that evening, and having been enticed to take too much. It did really seem for a little while as if grannie's death was to work good to him; for he would not go near the public-house, and he tried to keep out of the way of Mr. Simmons, and he attended Church quite regularly, like in old days.

But this did not last. Mother's influence was all a pull in the other direction, and grannie was gone, and I was but a child. And by-and-by father wanted more ready money, and he went again to Mr. Simmons, and after that the two were often to be seen together. Then the Church-going began to drop off again, and if I said a word about it father told me not to bother him, and he seemed never to like to speak about grannie.

Things were like this when the money came. For it came at last; close upon a year after old Morison's death. Not full five thousand pounds, though; for there was "legacy-duty" to be taken out of it, and that made a difference. And there were bills to be paid, and loans to be returned. Father and mother didn't like half so well paying the bills, as they had liked choosing things beforehand. And I am pretty certain Mr. Simmons must have made a nice sum for himself out of the lendings. He did not abate one penny of interest for the sake of friendship, as father had thought he would do; and father was so angry that he sheered off, and would have nothing to do with Mr. Simmons for a while. But he got over this feeling—more's the pity.

It is astonishing how the bills had run up—bills for food, and furniture, and dress, and all sorts of things. It was quite startling to us all. Father was very vexed, and he told mother it was all her doing, which made her cry. However, he finished off by saying that he didn't mean to be content with less than four hundred a year, but on four hundred he thought we might do grandly. So of course we might have done, if we had known how. But mother was comforted, and dried her tears, and neither seemed to care any longer.

I don't know who it was that father went to for advice about investing the money. I am quite sure it was neither Mr. Scott nor Mr. Carver, and just then father had quarrelled with Mr. Simmons; so it must have been somebody else. He told us he was to have near upon four hundred a year, and he seemed to think that would do anything.

The next step was that mother wanted Asaph to go to school, and to learn, as she said, "to be a gentleman." She chose a school where the terms were high, but neither she nor father minded that; only father said he did not see why I was not to go to school too. Mother said I was too old, and she wanted me in the house to help. Father gave in, and did not seem much to care, which disappointed me, for I should have liked school. Grannie had taught me to love books, and I always longed for more learning. I had to be content without, though, at that time.

A girl was hired, to work under me, and things were left pretty much in my hands, except that I never knew when mother would or would not give orders just opposite to what I had planned. It was well I had learnt to cook, for father was growing very particular in his eating, and mother gave no help, and the girl was idle and ignorant. There was no making her do things. After a while the girl was sent away, and an older servant was got in her place. She knew better what she was about, but she pleased herself as to what she did, and she was not at all a nice woman.

I missed grannie sorely those days. There was no one any longer to speak loving words to me; and there's nothing one misses like loving words, when one is used to them. Mother had never cared for me; and father was always grumbling.

Some days the weight on me seemed more than I could bear. There was no rule or order in the house; and how could there be? Mother took no heed to her duties as mistress; and the servant would not do as I wished. Everything was left to me, and I was blamed if things went wrong, and yet I had no power to make them go right.

I did so long for grannie back again. Life seemed dreary and sad without her. I remember one day meeting Mr. Scott, and his stopping to talk to me. He said so kindly, "Ah, it's a sad loss for you, poor girl!" And when I could not help crying, he took my hand and said, "But there is another Friend always at hand."

"But it does not seem as if I could be good without grannie," I said. "And I can't keep things straight. Nothing goes right now."

"She was one to help others," he said. "But there is nothing like looking to the Master Himself, Phœbe. Perhaps you didn't do that while you had her."

No; I did not, and I said so. I had always looked to grannie.

"I don't say that is why she was taken," he said. "I think God took her because He wanted her with Him in heaven. But now she is gone, I am quite sure He does want you to learn that lesson. Why should you not?"

"I don't seem to know how," I said, sobbing.

"Try—just try," he said. "Your grandmother was always near you, and always ready to help you. But there is One still more near, and still more ready. You turned to the one in every trouble; now turn to the Other just in the same way. And don't fear to trouble Him. Nothing that you care for is too small to pray about."

And then he said, "Your father has not been to Church lately."

"No," I said, and I blushed for him. "I can't get him to go, and he won't let me speak."

"Or your mother?"

"Mother doesn't seem to care," I said, and I hung my head.

"Don't let them keep you from God's House," he said.

"I do go in the evening," I answered. "Mother wants me at home all the morning. Father likes a hot dinner, and if I didn't see to it things wouldn't be right for him. Grannie never would do it, but mother makes me now."

"You are but a child," he said. "If they desire it, your duty may be for the present to yield. But if it is not needful, they ought to let you go. Some day I will call and perhaps speak about it."

And he did so, very kindly, but it wasn't of much use. Mother was angry, and after he was gone she said she would not be meddled with, and I was to do as she and father liked.

CHAPTER XIII

A Damp Dwelling

ONE gets used, more or less, to almost any sort of state; and by the time we had been seven or eight months in the house, I remember how things looked quite natural, and the old life in the cottage seemed almost like a dream to me. I don't know whether it did to the others. I am not saying that I liked the new life, or would have chosen it: but there it was, and one had to go through with it.

We had a great deal of pleasuring that summer. Everybody was very friendly; and I must say this for father, that having more money did not make him want to throw off old acquaintances, as some in his place might have done. It turned his head enough, but not in that way.

Father did not take to work again, and it is quite certain he was none the happier for being idle. It wasn't as if he had anything else to take the place of what he was used to do. I never saw any man change as he changed, month by month. The old brisk ways and pleasant look quite disappeared, and in their stead came a slouching sort of manner, and a lazy discontented expression. He was always grumbling and never satisfied; and he went to bed early, and got up late, and did not seem to know what to do with himself when he was up: and as for eating and drinking, they were getting to be the chief business of his life. I hope it isn't unkind to write all this, for how could I help seeing it? Mother fretted sometimes about the change in him, though she dearly liked being able to wear smart caps and dresses, and to show off before the neighbours how much money we had. She and Mrs. Raikes got into a sort of race, as it were, to see which should be the smartest. Each wanted to have the best parlour and the gayest clothes. Father laughed sometimes in a gruff sort of way, and said it was "folly," but he did not check it.

So for many months things went pretty smoothly. I had a sort of feeling, girl as I was, that all was not right: and yet I could not have told why, or have said where the wrong lay. Money seemed plentiful; or, if at times father ran short, he told us just to order things at the shops, and "next week" he would "make all square." I used to see mother getting all sorts of things for herself and Asaph and the house, but she seldom took me with her to the shops, and I could not tell what was paid for and what was not.

With the coming of autumn there seemed to come a dawning of trouble. The last half of the winter before had been very mild and very dry—two things not often seen together in an English winter—and we had not felt the dampness of our new house so as to be really inconvenienced. But this second winter came in quite differently. From very early autumn we had heavy rains, and cold winds, and sharp frosts, taking turns one with another. Water seemed to ooze in everywhere throughout the house, and rooms were damp, and cold could not be kept out.

Mother was the first to suffer. She had a desperately bad cold, which she could not shake off, and it came back again and again. She was very low-spirited about herself, and she said the damp of the house was killing her. She wanted father to have workmen in to put it all to rights. Father answered her quite roughly, and said he had no money to waste on such rubbish. That was the first time I heard him talk of being short of money.

Mother's cough grew worse, and the doctor had to be called in. He thought her in a bad way, and he said so pretty plainly, to mother's great terror. I don't know whether father would have taken warning then or not, but all at once he had a chill himself, and bad rheumatism came on in his back and arms, so sharp as well-nigh to cripple him for the time.

Father had not thought so much of mother's cough, but he thought a good deal of his own rheumatism, and he sent for the workmen in a hurry. A pretty mess they made, and a long while they were, opening walls, and pulling up flooring, and laying down pipes. And after all, the mischief was not cured. The very week after we got rid of them we had a day of pelting rain, and almost every wall in the house was running down again with damp. Mother could not sleep at night for her cough, and father was worse than before.

So the workmen came back, and I suppose they did their best; but the best was not much. Father said it was a downright badly built house, and he took to blaming mother for making him take it. Mother would cry and defend herself, and there was quite a bickering. Father had never been used to bicker in old days, but we had enough of it now. He was so often vexed and peevish that we did not know what to do with him—partly, perhaps, with the pain of his rheumatism, and partly with having nothing to do.

Mother found that an extra glass of beer sometimes made him more good-humoured for a little while, and she took to giving it him now and then. It was not her way to see dangers ahead, and father was easily persuaded. I did beg her not, but she said there was no harm, and she would not listen to me. It grew to be quite a common thing, when he was kept indoors by his rheumatism, to see him sitting with the tankard by his side, between meals. Mother never seemed to think that she was doing the Tempter's work. She just wanted to have things easy, and not to have him scolding her.

Christmas came, and I found it hard to believe that only one year had gone by since grannie's death. The time seemed so very much longer, and the months between had been so dreary.

And yet they were not altogether dreary. For it had been with me as Mr. Scott said,—the very fact that I had not grannie to look to had made me look more to God. I suppose that if she had lived

I should just have gone on leaning upon her, instead of leaning upon God. I did feel this Christmas that I had got on in the twelve months past,—that I seemed to know Christ more as my own Saviour, and that I cared more for doing His will, and that prayer was more of a needs-be in my life, or at least that I had learnt it to be so, and that my Bible was more dear to me. And it was not so hard, as once it had been, to keep from jealousy of Asaph and from impatience with others.

So Christmas came and passed away, and after Christmas the weather became fine and dry, and father and mother both seemed better in health. Father sat less indoors with his ale beside him; but I was afraid things were not really any more as they should have been. He found his way to the public-house oftener than he had ever been used to do; and sometimes he came home with a look in his face which I had seen, and shrunk from, many a time in other men.

C H A P T E R X I V

Christmas

CHRISTMAS bills came dropping in thick and fast that year. I had not looked for so many; neither, I am sure, had father and mother. It is so easy to order in a lot of things, each costing little enough by itself, without in the least knowing how much they will come to altogether.

Father began to get vexed, and to say, "What! another!" and a black look would come into his face. And sometimes he would stamp his foot and say, "Here's more of your extravagance, Sue! You'll ruin us all at this rate." And when mother said, "Why, Miles, what's a few shillings to us now? You've plenty of money!" he made answer. "Oh, have I though? I know better!" So I could see things were not all going straight.

From that time father made a sudden change in his way of speaking. Instead of always saying, as he had been used to do of late, "There's money enough,—never fear!" or "Do as you like,—thank goodness, I can afford it!" he twisted right round the other way, and was for ever repeating, "Can't afford this;" and "Can't afford that;" till mother declared we might just as well never have had the five thousand pounds at all. Not that I mean to say we really began even then to be careful. Father wouldn't have any difference made at dinner, for instance. He was never content without the best of everything there. And it seemed to me that whatever he wanted he got, and whatever mother wanted she got too,—only he said often that he could not afford things.

As for all the bills they were put into a drawer and just left alone there, as if they might be expected to pay themselves. But this of course could not go on. By-and-by they began to come in a second time, and father was spoken to by one tradesman and another in a way that he did not find pleasant. So, though he had begun of late to dislike any sort of work, and to find everything a trouble, except smoking and lounging about, he did at last actually look through the whole pile, and find out what they all came to, added up together.

Neither he nor mother had had before then any notion of how the prices of small things mount up. Mother was always saying, "Oh, it's only a shilling;" or, "It's only a half-crown;" or, "What's five shillings out of four hundred pounds?" And father and she had had no sort of steady plan in their spending, but had just got anything here and there as they felt inclined.

But four hundred a year will not buy everything,—no, nor four thousand either. And it seems to me that the question of being poor or rich don't so much hang on what a man has, as on what a man wants. He that has one hundred a year of money, and has wants that can be satisfied on ninety a year, is rich; and he that has five thousand a year, with wants that can only be satisfied on six thousand, is poor. I think we were poorer in our new home than we had been in the little cottage.

A good many bills had been allowed, the last Midsummer, to stand over till Michaelmas; and a good many more had been allowed to stand over till Christmas. It was no wonder that the tradespeople were getting impatient at last.

But I did not know how bad things were, till that day when I came into the parlour, and found mother crying. I had been helping to cook, and my hands were all floury. Mother often cried at little things, but this was something worse than common. I knew it in a moment from her face.

"What's wrong, mother?" I asked, and I shook the flour from my hands and came close to her.

"Matter enough," said she. "But it don't signify. You won't understand."

"Maybe I should," I said. "I am not a child now, you know."

"Aren't you?" she said, and she looked at me. "No, you are getting tall, to be sure. You're taller than me." And then she burst out crying afresh. "O Phœbe!" said she,—"father's been so awfully angry."

"What about, mother?" I asked.

"Why, about everything," said she, sobbing. "About everything, Phœbe. He says I'm ruining him, and it's all my fault if we can't pay our way, and he says I'm just worth nothing at all. I wonder whatever poor father would have said to hear him,—poor father as used to dote on me so. And I'm sure, if I have spent money, wasn't it Miles himself that told me to get whatever I liked? And now to have him turn on me like this."

"But what made father angry to-day?" I asked.

"Why, it's nothing at all," said she. "He's only just been looking at the bills. He said he'd see how much it was altogether, and it came to more than he looked to find. He did get in a fury. It made me feel so fluttery-like, I don't seem to have got over it yet, and my heart beats like anything. And it isn't my fault. I didn't know there were so many things not paid for. He was always telling me he hadn't got money in hand, so I could have things put down to him at the shops."

"How much is it altogether, mother?" I asked.

"I can't tell you," said she. "He frightened me so, I didn't half know what he was saying. He stamped at me as if he was mad. I don't know whatever I shall do. He isn't a bit like what he used to be. I always did say I had one of the kindest of husbands, and now he has never a pleasant word for anybody. I don't believe he cares for a single person in the world, so long as he gets what he wants for himself."

"Oh, I think he cares, mother," I said,—"only he doesn't know what to do about the bills."

"And I'm sure I don't know," said she fretfully,—"so it's no use his bothering me. I suppose they'll have to wait: for he says he's got nothing to pay them with. I almost wish the money had never come to us at all, if things are going to be miserable like this."

"Mother, I think it must be as grannie said," I half whispered. "We didn't all ask God's blessing with it."

"Oh, I don't know as to that," said she. "It's father's way of going on that makes things miserable. And he says he won't have me buy nothing again for ever so long,—and how I can manage—"

"I think you'll be able, mother, for you've got lots of things," I said; "I'll try to help you. I do wish father would have plainer dinners, for we spend a deal on eating."

And while we were speaking father walked in. He had a red and angry look still, and mother shrank away from him as if she was frightened.

"So you're talking it all over, are you?" says he roughly. "Now mind, Phœbe,—you're a sensible girl, and I look to you. If we go on another six months as we've been doing, I shall be ruined outright. D'you hear? We shall be ruined, stock and stone. D'you understand?"

Yes, I did; but I didn't see the need for him to shout at us like that. Words are strong enough, spoken quietly. But men often seem to think women can't be frightened into behaving themselves, without they're hallooed at.

"You've brought me into a pretty pickle, as it is," says he, looking at mother. "Why, my whole year's income, if I had it this moment, wouldn't do more than set us straight, and not a penny left for the year to come."

"Father, what are you going to do?" I made bold to ask. "Are the bills to be left unpaid?"—and I did not like the thought.

"No," said he gruffly. "There's some won't wait. I'll have to borrow. It's lucky I have a friend like Mr. Simmons."

"Oh, not Mr. Simmons, father!" said I.

"And why not?" says he.

I couldn't tell why. I could only say,—"I don't like him,—and grannie didn't either."

"Don't be a goose, Phœbe," said he. "Don't like him! What does that matter? I'm not asking you to like him. He'll lend me money to get over this, and that's all I want."

"Father," said I, "couldn't we begin to spend less, some way or other? If we were to have only a girl in the house, as we had at first—I'd work hard with her."

But mother said, "O no! Mrs. Raikes doesn't do with a girl." And father said, "Don't you meddle." So that shut my mouth.

C H A P T E R   X V

Trouble

So father borrowed from Mr. Simmons, and paid off the bills owing, and everything seemed straight again—only of course there was the interest to be paid to Mr. Simmons, making our income smaller.

I did think father and mother would learn wisdom from the past, but it was not so. Almost as soon as ever the thing was settled, father seemed to forget his anger, and mother seemed to forget her fear, and both went on just in the old way. I had no power, girl as I was, to check them. How should I have had? I saw things wrong, without the means of setting them right.

Months again went by—I do not know how many, for my memory is not quite cleat as to dates, but I know that as spring and summer passed we were getting afresh deeper and deeper into debt. I know that again and again father borrowed from Mr. Simmons, always at the same heavy rate of interest, and I know that the payment of this interest was becoming more and more of a drag upon us. Father never seemed to have money in hand for anything. He used to say, "Tell them to put it down to me, and I'll set it right next week."

But the tradespeople were gradually becoming a little shy of putting things down to father's name. I think it is likely they knew more than we did how father was going on, and how likely it was they might never get their money at all. Once when I wanted it done I was refused point blank, and when I told father he was quite in a fury. He said he should go to the shop and give them his mind; but I suppose he thought better of this, for he did not go. I found in time that there were a good many shops which father did not like to go near, and they were shops where he had heavy bills unpaid.

But still he and mother never drew in. It was always, "Oh, we must have this," "Oh, we can't do without that."

Father and Mr. Simmons were a great deal together. Father had nothing to do, and time often hung heavily on his hands; and yet he had taken such a hatred to work that he never would hear a word of doing any. But of course a man cannot spend his life in doing nothing, and so it came to pass that Mr. Simmons took to finding amusement for him. There were not many things that father could do, but he began to be more and more at the public-house and billiard-room.

Indeed, as months went by, we saw less and less of father. He was always with Mr. Simmons, and seldom came home except to dine and sleep. I think Mr. Simmons had the sort of mastery over him that a strong mind has over a weak one. Now and then they came in together, and I used to think of grannie's dread of Mr. Simmons, when I saw his smooth silky manners, and the sort of way in which he managed father, and made him do and say and even think just what he liked. But I could not venture on a word. Mother always seemed pleased to see Mr. Simmons. She did not in the least understand the harm he was doing.

Father had quite left off going to Church, and mother was seldom to be seen there either. They often laughed at me for being so regular, but I am thankful to say I never was even tempted to give it up. My chief comfort those days was in religion. I had nothing else. It was a life of hard slaving, with no love to cheer me in my work. Father was never satisfied, whatever I did.

It was through Mrs. Raikes that the whisper of how things really were first reached mother and me. She and mother were always trying still which could outdo the other, and they were in a sort of way at daggers drawn, if one may use the expression, though they didn't call themselves enemies.

Mrs. Raikes came in one day to see mother, with a fine wreath of red roses in her bonnet, which she had just bought—bigger and redder than one which mother had bought the week before. I suppose she came to show it off. I remember how her eyes spied all about our parlour, to see if there was anything in it new which she had not in hers. I wonder if I am uncharitable to write so. I know I am only saying simple truth; for she and mother used to boast and quarrel quite openly about which could be the smartest.

"Well," said she, "and what do you think of your husband being so mighty thick, as he has become of late, with that fellow Simmons?"

"Oh, Mr. Simmons and he are friends," mother said, tossing her head, "and I don't see why they shouldn't be, either. Mr. Simmons is an uncommon pleasant-spoken gentleman, and he's uncommon fond of my husband."

"Sooner your husband than mine," said Mrs. Raikes, and she gave a snort. "Raikes says to me once upon a time, says he, 'I'll bring Simmons home with me to dinner,' says he; 'I've met him, and I don't dislike him.' 'No, thank you,' says I; 'not if I knows it, Raikes. A mean sneaking cheat, as 'ud worm a secret out of a toad in a stone, and flay a man alive for sixpence. Not if I knows it,' says I. 'Why dear me, Kitty,' says he, 'whatever do you know of him?' 'Oh, you trust me,' says I; 'I've eyes and ears, I hope; and I know how to use 'em, too. No Simmons for me, if you please.' And Raikes he just laughed and didn't say another word. Oh, everybody knows what Simmons is at. And if you're not above taking a bit of friendly advice as it's meant, Mrs. Murdock, you'll do your best to get your husband out of his clutches."

It wasn't very likely, I suppose, that mother should be grateful for the advice, under the circumstances.

"I'm much obliged all the same," said she with another toss of her head. "I'm very much obliged all the same. But I hope my husband is free to choose his friends for himself, Mrs. Raikes. I'm not one of the wives that tyrannise over their husbands, like some. I'd scorn to have it said of Miles that he was a henpecked man. If it pleases him to make Mr. Simmons his friend, I'm very well pleased, and that's all about it."

"Well, I hope it may be all right," Mrs. Raikes answered. "I hope there mayn't be a deal to follow after, of a sort that won't be equally agreeable to you, Mrs. Murdock. Mr. Simmons is smooth-spoken enough, there's no denying; and he's clever at hiding his claws, there's no denying either. But when it comes to him and your husband—why, dear me, you don't suppose he'd ever have condescended to look at your husband, if it wasn't for the five thousand pounds."

"Maybe not," mother said shortly. "It does make a difference in our position, Mrs. Raikes, and everybody knows that."

"Oh, as for position, I'm not so sure," Mrs. Raikes said with a sniff. "A man's born one thing or another, and I don't see as a fuller purse alters him. But Mr. Simmons knows the worth of money, they say, and I don't doubt he'll make a paying business out of his friendship with your husband."

"I'm not at all afraid," says mother.

"Well, if folks won't take warning, they must be let to go on in their own way," said Mrs. Raikes. "I'm thankful it isn't my husband as spends his days gambling and drinking with Simmons. But if you're content, why it's no concern of mine."

"My husband don't gamble nor drink neither—much obliged all the same," says mother, getting very red.

"Oh, as for that, it's known to all the world, and anybody you like to ask'll say the same," Mrs. Raikes answered. "But I've no wish to vex you. It isn't my business. Only Raikes, he says to me this morning, 'That fellow Simmons will fleece Murdock of every penny he has,' says he. 'Couldn't you just give his poor wife a word of warning?' says he. And I says to him, 'I don't know as I dare, for she'll be out on me like a wild cat if I say a word; but maybe I'll try.' And now I've delivered my conscience, Mrs. Murdock, and I'd best say no more; only it's true enough all I've told you, and more's the pity."

And, when Mrs. Raikes was gone, how mother did cry! I never saw her cry so before. She wasn't afraid of many things that would frighten another wife; but she had a horror and dread of gambling, for she had seen the dreadful evil of it in her girlhood with a brother of her own.

C H A P T E R   X V I

Scenes

THAT very evening, strange to say, father came home the worse for drink. I had never seen him so bad, except the one night after grannie's death.

Somebody brought him to the door, and pushed him in and went away. I was almost sure it was Mr. Simmons, but I could not quite see in the dark, and he did not answer when I spoke.

I had to help father along the passage, and into the parlour; for he staggered and stumbled, and could not walk steadily. It was dreadful to me to have to do this. Such a feeling of shrinking and loathing came up in my heart, that I was frightened at myself. For it was my father—the father whom I had once loved so much, and who had been so good to us all. O what a change! To put himself down lower than a brute! All this was in my mind, as he came along, clutching at me for support, with his blood-shot eyes telling their tale.

And he was my own father. Such a great agony seemed to come up in my heart, that I felt as if I must rush away, and never see him again. But mother looked so frightened, standing apart, that I could not leave her.

"Phœbe! why, Phœbe, he has been drinking," she said quite loud. I wanted to silence her, but she said it again, and father heard. He had sense enough to understand, and he spoke angrily, using bad words, with his thick utterance.

It was no time for finding fault, but poor mother never was very wise in that way, and what was in her head came out at her lips. She burst into tears, and said, "Then it's all true, what Mrs. Raikes said; and he's been gambling too, I don't doubt. O Phœbe, Phœbe! what shall we do?" and she clung to me, as if for help; and I, poor helpless child that I was, with sobs half choking me, though I kept them down, did not know what to do.

Father heard the words, and he asked fiercely what they meant. Mother would not listen to me, when I begged her not to speak. She repeated what Mrs. Raikes had said, and then she told him he made her miserable, and was breaking her heart with his ways. She almost screamed out the words between her sobs, and father shouted back at her in a rage, though he could scarcely speak so as to be understood. It was a sad and grievous scene. Many and many a time I have envied those children who are so happy as not to know what it is to feel shame at their parents' actions.

I think I was praying in my heart, and a sort of calm seemed to come over me. I thought of what grannie would have done in my place. And I went to mother, and told her she must please not say another word, she must wait till next day. She left off then, and I told father he must go to bed. He stared at me, and then he went. I had to help him upstairs, and I thought we should never reach the top. He threw himself down all across the bed, with his clothes and boots on, and was asleep directly.

Mother would not go near him She came to my room, and crept into the bed with me. Neither of us could sleep much. I was very unhappy and cried a great deal; and yet I had a sort of pleasure in the thought that mother seemed to cling to me for help, in a way she had never done before.

The next day father was ill and miserable. He came downstairs late, and would take no breakfast, and sat crouching over the fire, and looked nobody in the face. Mother would not speak to him. It was a sad change from what our home had once been, and oh, I did feel thankful that dear grannie had not lived to see it.

Father got up after a while, and began to move off in a kind of slouching way. Mother spoke then. She called out in a sharp shrill voice which quite startled me, "Are you going back to your gambling?"

"Who told you I gambled?" said he angrily.

"Mrs. Raikes did," mother said. "And about your drinking too. I didn't believe neither; but now one's true, I suppose the other is true too. You'll just bring us all to the workhouse by-and-by, and that's what it'll be. That's how it is you never have a penny to spare for anybody's wants."

"Nor for squandering about your gewgaws of finery," growled he.

"A few shillings is nothing," said she. "But I know what it is, when a man takes to gambling. Haven't I seen it? And Mrs. Raikes says that man Simmons will fleece you of every penny; and I believe it too."

"Mrs. Raikes may attend to her own concerns," father said roughly.

"It's my concern too, though," mother said. "I should like to know how much you owe to Mr. Simmons."

"More than I'm like to be able to pay," father said in a sullen tone. "And I'd advise you to do nought to offend him, or he'll be down on us pretty sharp."

"Oh, that's the sort of friendship is it?" said she scornfully. "That's all it is worth. If I was you, I'd pay him back, and get rid of him, and never see him no more."

"O yes, you women are uncommon wise," said he, with a sneer. "A nice lot of finery you'd be able to get yourself, if I did that."

"Mother would sooner do without the finery, and have you free from Mr. Simmons," I said. "Wouldn't you, mother?"

"Yes, I would," said she.

Father went off without another word, and mother and I talked things over together. She seemed to find it a comfort, and I think she was at last willing to be careful, and to spend less on herself. But if father was really gambling away money to Mr. Simmons, nothing we could do would stop him.

So for the second time father had come home, the worse for drink. The first and second times had been far apart, but the second and third were near together, and the third and fourth nearer still; and soon we knew that it was getting to be a common event.

Things looked sad indeed, as Christmas once more came slowly round. Mother seemed so shocked and sobered, as to put aside her flightiness and to want to be different. She clung to me a good deal, and was willing to do anything I thought best. We sent away the servant, and had quite a young girl instead; and mother and she and I managed all between us. If the house had been smaller, we could have done without a girl even, only I don't think father would have been willing.

Mother was far from strong that winter. The damp tried her again, and her cough was often very bad.

It was strange to me to see how all this seemed to be taking effect on her, and how much less she cared about dress and show than she had done. One Sunday she suddenly said she thought she would go to Church again, and when she came back she had been crying. After that she scarcely ever missed going: once each Sunday. And sometimes at night, when we were waiting and watching for father to come home, she would let me read the Bible to her.

I was so glad that Asaph was away at school, and I did dread his coming home at Christmas, and seeing what father was come to. It would be so terribly bad for him, I thought. But a change came before Christmas, sudden and unexpected.

CHAPTER XVII

The End

ONE evening, about ten days before Christmas, mother and I were waiting, as we so often did, for father's return. It was earlier than he commonly came back, so we did not expect him yet. I had been reading to mother the fifteenth of John, and she said she did wish she had cared more for such things. She thought, if she had, she would be happier. And I said it wasn't too late, for God was always willing to answer if we asked Him.

And then, all at once, there was a great noise and banging at the front door. I went out to see what it was, and some men came in, carrying a helpless body.

I remember shivering with the old feeling of horror and dread, not of fear. I thought he had taken too much again.

And so he had, but that was not all. He had fallen into a cellar, and was very much hurt. The men spoke as if they scarcely knew whether he still breathed.

It was terrible indeed. I called mother, and she shrieked and wrung her hands and seemed half beside herself. There was no learning particulars at first. Father was carried upstairs, and laid on the bed, and one of the men went off for a doctor.

Father lay quite quiet and senseless, not even moaning. Dickenson, our former neighbour, was one of those who had come, and I took him aside, and asked how it had all happened.

He could not tell me very much. Partly from what he had seen, and partly from what had been told him, he knew that father had been with Mr. Simmons in the billiard-room, and that they had been playing for money, and that father seemed to lose over and over again and was very much excited, while Mr. Simmons seemed trying to soothe him. Then the two went into another room, and drink was called for, and father became still more excited. He seemed trying to get up a quarrel with Mr. Simmons, and he said over and over again that Mr. Simmons had ruined him.

Mr. Simmons kept quite cool all the time, but presently he was seen to get up and move away, in a sort of stealthy manner, making believe that he was coming back directly. Father grew quite furious then, and attacked him with his fists, and others in the room had to come to the rescue. Mr. Simmons took himself off, by their advice, and seemed not at all sorry to do so; and father went back to his seat, muttering and grumbling, and saying "he would be even with him yet."

After a while he got up to go home, and Dickenson, seeing how unsteady he was, followed some distance behind, not feeling sure that help mightn't be needed. And so it was. Father had not gone half a street length, before he seemed to fancy he saw Mr. Simmons ahead. He set up a sort of shout, and rushed off at a blind pace, and in a moment went headlong down a kind of open trap-door, with a deep warehouse cellar below. The marvel was that he escaped death on the spot.

I went back to him, after hearing all this, and waited till the doctor came. Mother was sobbing and crying and would not stay in the room. I did not dare to touch father. He lay just as they had put him down, helpless and senseless. Sometimes I thought he must be already gone. The men were very good, and would not leave me alone. One was Sykes, Mr. Johnstone's foreman, and I never shall forget his kindness, as he tried to cheer me up.

When the doctor came, I was sent away, and there was a long examination. Mother was sobbing so as to be quite useless, and the doctor sent for me afterwards, to speak to me.

He said that father was terribly hurt. There were broken bones, but he feared these were not the worst injuries. He could not say more yet, however: so he only gave careful directions how I was to manage, and promised to come again next day.

The next few weeks were just one long bout of nursing. It was wonderful how good some of our old neighbours were,— those who had been grannie's friends in earlier days. As for newer friends, who had clustered round us when the money came, they dropped off like dead leaves from a tree in autumn.

I don't know what we should have done without help. Mother was such a poor nurse, and so easily overcome, and also she was in sickly health. And I was a mere girl, quite unused to illness.

As the weeks passed on, father did not seem really better. The broken bones were mending, but he lay still like a log, seeming to have no power in his body and no sense in his mind. At first there was a great deal of fever, and his thoughts wandered much; but when that passed off, sense did not come back. He knew nobody clearly, and was like a little child, having to be fed and cared for every hour.

And at last the doctor told us plainly that it always would be so. He said he had feared it from the beginning. The injuries to the head and spine were so great that father could never recover from them. He might linger on a good many years, but he would be helpless and childish to the end.

I can see now how this great trouble was sent in mercy to mother and me, for we were saved by it from greater miseries. But at the time we could not see things so. When we thought how the accident had happened, and when we remembered what father had once been, it seemed almost more than we could bear.

For a long while there was no time to think of anything but the nursing. Soon, however, it became needful to give attention to something else. Christmas bills had come in again, and tradespeople were growing impatient. And when mother and I began to look into the matter, we found strangely little of the five thousand pounds left. Father had been selling out capital again and again, unknown to us; so instead of £400 a year there was not £200, and there were demands enough to swallow up a good part of what remained. Mr. Simmons had fleeced poor father indeed; though of course it had not all gone in that direction.

Mr. Simmons was nowhere to be found. He had gone away a day or two after the accident, to pay a week's visit to a friend,—so he said. But though a good many weeks had gone by, he had not returned, and he never did return. Nobody knew his whereabouts: so we could ask him no questions about father's affairs.

We let our house as quickly as possible, and we sold out a good part of what remained of the money, so as to pay off everything. Mother said I should manage it all my own way, and I could not bear to keep people waiting longer for their due. I went to kind Mr. Scott, and he helped me with advice. Then we settled to live in a tiny cottage, much smaller than our old one, which had a second room on the ground-floor, beside the kitchen, where father could sleep. There was just enough money left to keep us going, with great care, and with the help of what we could earn,—I by charing, and mother by needlework. Asaph came to live at home, and went to a shop every day as errand boy.

These changes were at first a great trouble to mother. Yet in time she learnt to be thankful that she had not been left to go on in her old way, caring for nothing but amusing herself. And as for me, I was far happier in the little cottage than I had been in the house.

Not that there was any harm in our having a nice house and more money, if God gave them to us. The harm was in taking it all, without a thought of how to use and spend according to His will.

Father never became better. He lived some years, always in the same state. He had hardly more sense than a baby, and did not seem to remember the past. I often said to him texts and easy hymns, but I never could tell if he understood. He passed away suddenly at last, in his sleep. Ah,—he was a sad wreck. Things might have been so different with him!

We three lived on long together in the little cottage, afterwards; and Asaph grew to be our comfort and stay. The change came only just in time to save our boy from being quite spoilt. But father's state was a sharp warning to him. He seemed to become more thoughtful from that Christmas—and no wonder.

THE END